What Love Can't Do

A Novel by Kitty Beer

Plain View Press
P. O. 42255
Austin, TX 78704

plainviewpress.net
sbright1@austin.rr.com
512-441-2452
512-440-7139 (fax)

for Duncan and Amelia

"The green globe's broken; vines like tangled veins
Hang at the entrance to the silent wood."
— from "On Winter's Margin"
by Mary Oliver

Episode 1

I'm Not Going Without You

"They're circling the house."

Looking out the back window, she can just make them out in the dusk. Leon, stirring the stew, drops the spoon and comes to stand behind her.

"I had thought they were just passing by," Tati says, trying to calm the pitch of her voice.

Ten of them, so young, with their wild hair and costumes yellow and black, their colors, loping along in their furtive feral way.

"They're just babies, younger than our children," he says into her hair. "Fourteen, sixteen, tops."

"They see us. They're glad we're watching. What do they want?"

Leon doesn't need to answer. They both know what the gang wants. Food and water, and a little blood fun perhaps.

It's been six months since he came to her door, Leon. Unbathed, distraught, he'd had to abandon his car twenty miles earlier. The severe April sun had caked his lips and he croaked when he greeted her. "Used to know your brother Ned," he stated, as if she should believe him, a crazy looking stranger, and she a woman all alone except for her delirious ancient father upstairs dying and Fox, just a pint-sized dog.

She came out on the porch, blocking the door, Fox barking gratifyingly in the background.

"I brought you some honey cakes, your favorite."

She looked at the battered package, up at his gray stubble, earnest exhausted dark eyes hopeful. Who else but Ned could have told him about her craving for honey cakes? Avoiding his acrid smell, she stepped well away, gestured him in. Sat him down at her kitchen table, where he gulped water, bread and cheese. Wrapped herself anew in the grief of Ned's death along with their mother's in the malaria epidemic of the 2030s, the shared pain a comfort in this lonely dangerous zone where she existed, day to deadening day.

Later, Leon emerged from a bath glowing and almost cheerful, thin hair slicked back, freshly dressed in one of her father's shirts. Face worn and weather beaten and groove lined as a walnut shell, shoulders stooped, an old goat. But she noticed his broad expressive hands, weaving gestures, gripping his cup, and found herself thinking vaguely of caresses. Tati was no stranger to desire. But it had been so long...years...she was startled to recognize the signs.

His own passion was all directed at getting back on the road. Finding his family — two sons, a grandchild. He was on his way north from Pennsylvania to Canada, ran out of gas just outside Dedham, had to walk all the way here to Concord. She couldn't help him with that, of course; gasoline was nowhere to be found. But she thought she might know a group leaving soon, in a solar-powered camper. Everyone was leaving, pouring north to escape the implacable heat and the drought and disease that come with it. Tati's own daughter Crea had settled near Montreal three years before, and Tati would be with her today if it were not for Ray, who just kept on dying and never would get it over with.

"This is my father Ray." She introduced him to Leon as if it were a social occasion, as if the old man were not lying there in the shadows smelling like rotting flesh, each breath like his last, staring wildly at them both as if they were phantoms. "Daddy, this is Leon, an old friend of Ned's."

Leon stepped to the bedside and grasped her father's limp hand in greeting.

"Ned? Ned, win the soccer game, Ned." Ray's papery voice was urgent. "Good boy."

Tati gently lifted his head to adjust the pillow. Standing there beside Leon she felt a surging transfer of energy. All the life her father had been draining from her was replenished and she felt full, gorged, absurdly, rebelliously alive.

"Sure, Dad," said Leon tiredly but with kindness. "I'll win the soccer game. I'll win it for you."

But if she thought that Leon would rescue her from despond, it was not to be. At first she was lonelier than ever, as he immersed himself in his obsession with collecting and assembling the fuel cells he needed for his car, or just guarded himself with little repair tasks about the house. Even after they found each other's bodies, and it became clear that he wanted to linger here in her embrace, he was often off in a dream place, and he hated it when she talked about her sadness. She learned to hide behind smiles and kisses, to only obliquely try to reach his heart.

Now by the window watching the dangerous children in the twilight, Tati closes her eyes for a second, leans back into him, the comfort of his always warmth, to better feel his groin against her, escaping just for a moment into their own blind sensual place where nothing else can touch them.

Leon puts his arms around her, says, "Come on, let's forget about them."

Dropping the curtain, she turns into his embrace. She's tallish, still with an angular mold in spite of the weight gains that in recent decades have thickened her waist, puffed her belly, fleshed out her face so that her small nose and mouth now look too small. Grey hair long enough to be clipped up at her neck, often with the amber clasp that Crea gave her one birthday, long ago.

Crea standing in the kitchen laughing the way they used to be able to — freely, fully — lifting Tati's then autumn gold hair in her hands. As Tati felt the scoop of her daughter's touch on her neck, her heart tightened. Is it her memory or the truth that even in that sweet lost time her rush of love whispered a warning chill? Back then they still had no idea what was to come, though why didn't they? The signs in the 20s were everywhere.

"That's odd," Crea commented one May morning. "The robins haven't come this year."

As he kisses her, Leon lifts Tati's dress and takes deft fingers to her thighs. Her mind numbs willingly. Their little moans are a chorus of defiance.

After nightfall it rains. It rains the way it usually does these days, desperately, piteously, slanting hard, pummeling the dirt but never soaking it, mud rivulets evaporating. The next morning, even though they go out not long after dawn, everything is dry again. Fox hysterically finds the heads and bones of squirrels, freshly strewn. No evidence of fire, what would they burn anyway? "Suppose they have a solar cooker?" "Doubt it." That the children probably ate the animals raw goes unsaid.

Leon also finds a straw bracelet, woven and worn. Between aversion and sorrow, Tati says, "It's so terribly small."

Today they have to go out for food. They admonish Fox to keep guard, and stride out along the street past the mostly deserted houses wearing their backpacks and wide-brimmed hats.

"You don't have to stay." Tati starts tentatively, ready for his terse response.

"We've been through this."

"You could've been there by now. The families with that camper are there now."

As she pursues this argument more earnestly than she has for some time, she becomes aware that her purpose now is not so much to draw assurance of his affection as to combat despair.

"You've got the car back now, and the cells to run it — at least until Burlington. If it weren't for my father…"

"Of course we'll wait."

"I could join you later."

"That's it, Tatyana. Shut up, my sweet. You're not getting rid of me."

He squeezes the nape of her neck with a quick assertive caress. His eyes are shadowed under the hat, his smile tight. He hasn't wanted to understand that she is losing hope.

They come out on the highway that leads to 95 North, climb down to a path to avoid the traffic all streaming in one direction, a bizarre assortment of vehicles, from the strange camel-humped "cooking oil campers" to wagons pulled by horses or bicycles. Here and there a vintage car from the old days, gaped at by the others. Or at least by those whose heads are not bowed, exhausted and uncaring. Except for the occasional clank or whine of a makeshift engine, there's a chilling quiet, just the shuffling of feet. Even now, well before noon, the clouded sky gives no respite from the boiling sun. Along the path lie people already overcome, sprawled in what meager shade they can find. If their water has run out, they'll have none until they reach the fetid swamp of Walden Pond.

Leon and Tati pass through a swath of trees that still look healthy, crowns intact. In here, where for a moment even the air is different, ghosts of the lost green world arise.

The summer she graduated from college she was living at home, in the shabby grandiose house she loved and hated, with her silly mother who was dating yet another unemployed genius. Ned was off visiting their father in Montauk. Tati was having a fling with an old boyfriend from high school, throwing herself into their imaginative lovemaking in offbeat places with regressive abandon. A favorite nook was in the grass behind her old playhouse shielded by lush lilacs and shaded by a giant oak. One morning when she was sleeping even later than usual, she woke to the high-pitched whirr of chainsaws. At first she thought it must be the next-door neighbor obsessing over his bushes, but the noise was too loud for that. Finally she dragged on her robe and went outside to the back deck. Just on the other side of the fence where towered the oak, at least a hundred years old, two men straddled the broadest branches. The crown was already gone, all the leaves and the lesser branches. They were savaging the tree with the bravado of cowboys killing buffaloes. She ran out screaming at them, but of course it was too late. Even if they had stopped, the tree could never survive without its crown. And anyway, the neighbor owned the tree and had a perfect right, in those days, to get rid of it.

"Do you remember," she says dreamily, "how the trees used to be?"

Leon doesn't answer. He's keeping an eye on the path ahead as it comes to an abrupt end at the scarred asphalt of the abandoned mall.

So she murmurs to herself, "Crea says there are still plenty of trees in Terrebonne."

The long expanse of concrete is pocked with fissures sprouting yellowed grass and vines. The M of a McDonald's tips on its side to form a Greekish E. Some of the windows in some of the stores are broken, but there is no sense of violation, just a blank, a deletion. At the end of the old parking lot they have to climb back up to cross the highway to another road. On their way across they watch a pickup truck being pulled by a motorcycle. In the back of the truck nestled in a pile of furniture under a makeshift canopy squat three grimy children, who wave at them.

After passing the fish farm — miles of oblong, sluiced ponds in a grid — they reach the market place. Besides fish they load up with greens, radishes, apples, potatoes, goat cheese, canned milk.

"Looks to be a late winter," croaks ancient Andrew pleasantly, trussing up the groceries in the backpacks.

"At least we won't need as much fuel," Leon obliges in the same conversational tone.

No room for despair here, no voice for it.

"Be thankful for small blessings," Andrew chuckles, as always.

Tati smiles at him warmly, meaning it.

When they get home, Fox dashes down the stairs from Ray's room, his overlarge feathery tawny ears sailing behind him, effervescence signaling an uneventful watch. Tati follows him back up to find her father in a peaceful sleep. She adjusts the sheets, dabs away sweat from his forehead and neck. If only he would die, so they could leave, so she and Leon could go north to find their children and something like a normal life. She is angry with her heart because it is so full of love for this crumpled wreck clinging absurdly to a remnant of life, blocking her escape.

While Leon tries to fix some damaged solar panels, Tati bleeds the rainwater barrel, boils and filters water, scrubs potatoes. After lunch they lie down in bed together, intertwined, exhausted from the heat and the laborious trip.

"Do you suppose they'll come back tonight?"

"They'd just be passing through," Leon assures her. "Why would they stay?"

As she falls asleep, Tati thinks he must be right, and knows he is not.

A prolonged gurgling shriek shocks them awake. The unearthly sounds from Ray are joined by primeval howls from Fox. They race up the stairs to find Ray on the floor, vomiting blood.

Tati cries out, kneels in the red pool.

"No, no," orders Leon. "Let me lift him back up. Let go of him."

But she keeps her father's head in her arms as he struggles to breathe in blood, coughs it out, breathes it in. She watches his contorted face freeze, wildly searches his staring eyes for recognition, for some return on her love.

With sunset comes a fiercely beautiful rose light. Leon is doing all the packing while Tati sits on their bed, sapped by roiling tears. In the next room Ray lies washed, wrapped, ready to be buried in the morning. Now they can leave, she thinks, tries to exult. He's dead so now they can go, at last. And it's getting more and more dangerous here. She didn't like the looks of that band last night, the most daring and menacing group yet. Hornets, they call themselves, like the children they are, all got up in their team colors yellow and black, macabre Halloween. Waves of them

on their way north, now sometimes as many as twenty to a gang. The gun
is propped against a wall in the basement. It's not loaded, but the bullets
are there in a box. Ray's old rifle. When did he last clean it? Would she or
Leon be capable of firing it at human beings, even if only to scare them?
She gets up and goes downstairs to the back door.

The yard is cooling in the purpling light. The old maple is toughing
it out, still mostly green, casting long shadows. Bunches of orange mari-
golds bloom valiantly in its shade. Of course the vegetable garden is long
stripped bare, by the first Hornets who found it in the spring. Tati is a good
shot. Ray taught her and Ned the summer she was fourteen, targeting empty beer cans in the pond. Her father was proud. She won stuffed animals at
fairs.

It was the last summer they were together as a family. Ray left right
after Christmas, Tati never really understood why. Her mother was flighty,
dreamy, prone to hysterics, but pretty and sweet. He'd begun to make tons
of money in one of those new internet companies that were springing up
in the 90s. But still, why not keep his charming and affectionate wife?
Now, of course, Tati will never be able to ask him.

So there they all were that August, renting a cottage on a pond near
Eastham, Cape Cod. At fourteen, Tati was undergoing turbulence of her
own. She wanted Tommy Tolman to kiss her. This eventually happened,
when she least expected it, in the back of the car driving home from a
movie. Something glistened on her shoulder — Tommy's watch. Before
she quite realized this meant his arm was around her, his lips were on her
cheek. In slow magical motion she turned her face to meet his mouth. She
felt the heat of his tongue down to her belly. That was it; she was sold on
love.

"C'mon, Ned," Ray said, "you've got to learn about guns, son."

Piqued, Tati pouted, "I want to learn too, Dad," although she certainly
didn't.

But the feel of the long cold metal was somehow satisfying, and watching her father's deft hands loading and unloading, admiring her capable
own, and aiming out over the tranquil pond, the ping of hitting the target,
the thrill of his praise.

She had gone back to that pond once since, when Crea was about
twelve. They had to go by boat, of course, with half the Cape under water
by then. Her husband had refused to come — he was always too depressed
for adventures. The pond was dead, salinated by the encroaching sea. She
crouched on the shore and wept. So the memories of that last family summer became distorted, overlaid with the pitiful sight of the encrusted pond.

Tati goes out into the yard, barefoot in the dusty grass. On the trunk of
the old tree is a snail the size of a walnut. Its gray oozy body is just visible
beneath its spiral home and its long rubbery antennae look vulnerable as

skinless flesh. The antennae have little knobs at the end that tremble and vibrate. This morning the snail had been clinging a few inches from the bottom of the tree; now its daylong journey has brought it to the height of her chest. It has a purpose, pursues it. Tati thinks, how does my life make any more sense than this one? What's the use?

She hears Fox start to bark from inside the house, turns and is face to face with a Cheshire grin under a forest of mangy hair knotted with feathers.

"We wants the dawg."

His voice is a soft drawl. In a paralyzed second she stares at him realizing, then turns and runs, so fast that she has locked the door before she feels her feet racing. Palm on the window she sees him still standing there under the tree, laughing. Leon and Fox tear into the kitchen — was she screaming? Others now are loping towards the tree and he's telling them the joke, the shit-scared lady joke, and they all are laughing and leering back at the house. Tati is trembling so hard she would fall if Leon were not holding her. Fox is wailing hysterically. The Hornets bunch into a kind of parade and saunter around the side of the house towards the front.

"Did he hurt you?"

She shakes her head, buries herself in Leon's embrace. She drinks the water he gives her, leans down to pick up Fox.

"The car," Leon says.

Outside the front window the sky keeps only a slash of mauve light just behind the dark houses across the street. The car is parked in the driveway. It's a reddish color, maybe ten years old, with the dolphin shape peculiar to 2030 models. A carrier wagon is hitched to the back for a few pieces of furniture as well as bedding, dishes, clothes. Leon has already stacked it with a table and some chairs, a rug. The Hornets dance around it, gesticulating.

"Leon, they'll take it!"

"No. Fuel cells not in yet."

"But what if they destroy it? We can't leave without the car. We can't leave."

Tati's panic tastes bitter, like nausea rising. She is clutching her elegant rose colored drapes in both hands as if to squeeze life from them. The Cheshire man does a gazelle leap ending in an obscene gesture, then leads the parade on around the house towards the back again. They are chanting something. As they disappear, the words float back.

"We wants dawg blood, dawg blood, dawg blood."

The Hornets continue circling the house, doing little dances that imitate dogs, hanging their hands like paws and cantering. Leon lights lamps and starts up the stove. Cradling Fox, Tati watches him. He's going to start cooking, he's going to pretend this is normal.

Fox follows her down into the basement. She finds the rifle easily, but has to scramble around to find the ammunition. She loads awkwardly but without hesitation. Fox sits very quietly. He knows something is wrong. She smoothes his silky head and meets his eyes.

"Don't worry," she tells him. "I'll kill them first."

When she appears with the rifle, Leon chuckles anxiously.

"Annie Oakley."

But she strides past him to the window.

"You're not, Tatyana, you're not serious…."

The Hornets are not in the back yard. As Tati heads for the front of the house, Leon following in alarm, they hear a crash. In the driveway the gang has formed a half circle near the car, piles of rocks at the ready. The car's rear window is splintered. Seeing them watching, Cheshire man waves, all the wild creatures wave, pick up rocks and dance with them, chanting.

"Give us the dawg, give us the dawg."

Tati opens the window and fires over their heads. Stunned, they freeze. In their wild clothing, in their various poses, in their amazed, angry faces, for a split second they appear disembodied, a work of art in progress. Then a rock comes through the window of the house, slamming into the wall just beyond Leon. Tati fires again, and again. Now the Hornets are scattering like leaves. The street is suddenly deserted. There is absolute silence in the darkness.

When a little later Tati and Leon venture outside to check on the car, they find the girl. She is unconscious, bleeding from a wound in her leg. A slip of a girl not more than fifteen, with an ashen baby face, her tangled hay colored hair shrouded around. Her suit of loose black is swathed at the waist with sharp yellow. Leon has the presence of mind to seek out a plank to lay her on. They carry her into the living room, drape a blanket over the couch. They work off the girl's trousers. The wound doesn't look bad, but how would they know? Leon learned CPR as a teenager and that's the medical training between them. The girl's underpants are worn but clean. They have little sheep designs on them, faded pink and blue.

"Won't they come back for her?"

" I don't know." Leon shakes his head sadly. "Look at how thin she is."

"I hope to God the bullet's not inside. Let's hope it just grazed her. Oh God, I didn't mean to hit anybody!"

The girl grimaces and opens her eyes, starts to cry.

"It hurts, it hurts," she whimpers, twisting in pain.

They give her aspirin and whiskey, that's all they have. They know enough not to try to scare up help this time of night.

"We'll have to take her with us," Tati whispers.

"Of course."

They spend the night packing. Dawn is grandiose, mocking in its glorious announcement. In the lavender glimmer they bury Ray.

The girl takes some water, then some juice, then is persuaded to chew a little bread. Her eyes are hard, meeting theirs in a cold stare. But she tells them her name.

"Trewth."

"Truth," replies Tati. "What a lovely name."

They bed Truth down in the back of the car nested in pillows and blankets with an uneasy Fox. She seems much better and they are hopeful.

At the highway they merge with the incessant parade northward.

Tati turns to smile at Leon. "So, six months later…"

"Six months with you. What a gift."

"Remember how desperate you were to get back on the road?"

"That didn't last long. You mesmerized me."

Tati looks out at the surrounding faces grim and wan.

"I wonder if," she says, "even though we didn't know it wishing so hard all the time to leave, I wonder if that was the last joy."

Episode 2

Refuge

"I want you to marry me."

She lies there in the silken warmth of their bed, damp with the liquid he has just spilled into her, looking up at him. He has stopped buttoning his shirt, for emphasis.

"I want you to marry me," Han repeats, with an edge. "We belong together."

His shirttails are hanging over his briefs. His legs just the right length for his tall frame, just the right amount of muscle, just the right amount of dark hair flecks. She meets his eyes.

"Isn't it too soon? It's hardly been a year...."

"It's been almost two years since he died, Crea. Don't tease me."

He turns his back. He's pulling on his trousers, roughly.

"Fair needs a little more time. She adored her father."

Her tone has taken on the pleading whine she hates, and he loves.

"Of course, darling." Now he sits on the bed, caressing her hair, breast. "Say, in a month, in March."

"A springtime wedding," she murmurs, curling towards him. "The spring of 2043, it even sounds romantic. Oh, Han, how lovely."

He rewards her with the tender kisses reserved for her submission. His mouth lingering pressure on her eyelids, neck, lips, heat that kindles her belly in spite of herself.

When he leaves, she turns to the blue morning light at the windows, the spray of black tree branches. An enormous nest — a crow's or a squirrel's — looms jauntily in a clutch of twigs. Still tenaciously there after the raging storms of the last week. Faintly comes piano song, Fair's morning practice. The elegant wisps of music from a distant peaceful time help her tears that blur the tree and sky. She'll have to tell Marcel.

After washing — using so much water that Marguerite the housekeeper fumes — she stands by the window. The fence is finally complete, shutting out the rabble from the broad lawn. All at once, there is the mysterious little old woman again, more visible now that she must stand inside the fence, a dark, brooding waif. She's incongruously wearing big black rubber boots, dwarfing the rest of her. White face tilted up to quiz the windows of the house. Many mornings now she lurks there, but not hiding, proud. Why don't they drive her off?

Fair at the piano glances up to smile at her mother, missing a note and pounding the next one vengefully. Such a lovely little girl, barely eleven, with burnt-red curls and delicate features. Such a determined little girl, out to fight her demons. A fierce little girl.

Marguerite tries to persuade Crea not to go out today.

"I've got to go to work," Crea insists.

"No, no. You won't go down to the lake flats! The streets are all flooded. The refugees are dangerous." Marguerite rants in her flamboyant French Canadian way, Latin with passion. "What will Captain Hanley say? You'll catch a cold, it's too difficult…"

"Thanks, Marguerite. I'll be fine."

Wearing a slicker and boots Crea takes off on her bike, down the hill towards the town. Because she must see him. Her job could wait until tomorrow, could wait for days. No one at the Guardian office would consider it odd for her to stay home in the aftermath of such a storm. But she needs Marcel, like oxygen.

The road at the bottom of the hill is clogged with them, families and their belongings crammed into assorted vehicles — wagons pulled by horses or motorcycles, oddly crafted conveyances lashed to bicycles or wheelbarrows, here and there an old car. They're all headed north, and Crea is headed across through the town center, so she manages to ride past them fairly fast, splashing through pockets of muddy water. One stark-eyed woman carrying a baby is wearing a once beautiful coat in tatters, muddied shoes without toes. The baby is screaming, but nobody seems to notice.

Word is they'll close the border soon. Thousands of these Americans are streaming across into Canada every day now, driven by the heat and drought, poisoned air and water, impending chaos. Their dream is the northern wilderness, but there are too many of them already, and even those newly settled want to stop the surge.

Crea manages to follow behind a convoy of Guards, trucksfull of hearty men in gray-blue uniforms. She waves to Lieutenant Renaud and he salutes with a smile. She's one of their own — she belongs to Hector Hanley.

Speeding past the lakefront shacks still flooded by the wild rains, past the marketplace, the computer café, and on up the next hill. Across from the church, Marcel's little storefront manages to look jaunty in spite of peeling paint. As she passes, she imagines she glimpses him among his paraphernalia: redeemed clocks, toasters, TVs, coffee pots, lamps. Dark hair falling aslant over his forehead, square sure hands adjusting some intricacy of screw or bolt. The nape of his neck.

The Guardian office is operating at a high pitch. Two days were lost because of the storm, and today at noon is the deadline. Crea plunges into the pile on her desk searching for an acceptable story. Fuel cells have been recharged and her computer is working. So she begins, "Bake Sale Features Giant Gingerbread Castle."

Shortly after noon she's walking as casually as she can down to Marcel's shop. Sunlight sparkles the lake. In the distance the worm of refugees along the road appears benign, almost peaceful.

She goes around to the back door and waits in the room where he lives. Table and chairs, couch, cooking range, ladder to sleeping loft. Her first time here she had been aware only of gratitude that she didn't have to live cooped up in a place like this — such a spare, shabby, cramped corner smelling old. She'd sipped warily at the tea he gave her, with a vague dismay that bordered on repugnance. But she kept coming back. His tirades excited her: against the authorities, the "bull-headed" Guards, the "despotic and inept" government, the "blind idiocy" of 20th century industries that had poisoned the Earth, the new Zorian religion ("cult crap") that everybody was falling for. She loves his anger. She wishes she could be angry.

Now she seeks him out for more reasons than she cares to admit. She's drawn here like someone in a fever seeking clarity. He wakes her from a dream.

She can hear him in the front room chatting with a customer, saying goodbye, closing and locking the door, its bell chiming. In a moment he'll be here, already she's warm with him.

When David died, Crea and Fair mourned among strangers, in a strange land. They had just crossed the border from Vermont a few days before. One morning he was a vibrant vigorous young man, by afternoon a gray depleted ghost, by nightfall dead. They buried him just outside Montreal with the countless other cholera victims. They tried to mark the spot, but they'll never be able to find it again.

Captain Hanley saw her a few weeks later standing in line for travel documents. Froth of pale blond hair countered by brown eyes, wide welcoming mouth countered by thin aloof nose, body round and lithe at once — her beauty a sum of contradictions. He ordered his sergeant to devise a problem, and she was brought before him. Already fragmented by grief, and now faint with new fear, Crea cowered by his desk. He was enthralled.

To Fair, Han is their hero. One day they were languishing in a crowded smelly tent with dozens of other miserable refugees, the next they were installed in a luxurious suite with running water and more food than she'd ever seen. She adapted with amoral speed, taking to fine living with nonchalant ease. By the time the child dimly realized, months later, that Han was in the process of taking her father's place in their lives, she was too far transformed to object. Anyway, her heart is closed and locked, her father safe inside.

Crea's heart is not so secure. While she watches Marcel stoke his stove, she knows that her eyes are resting too long on his shoulders, his hands.

"Marcel."

But, on his knees jabbing the coals, caught up in his perpetual fury, he misses her urgent tone.

"Don't see how they can police that whole border," he growls. "Sure, conscription's gone from two to three years now, but they'll need every man and woman just for that. They'll have to start shooting people."

"Hopefully not," she murmurs.

She's slicing the cheese she brought, standing at his little table. The room is so small they're barely four feet apart. He slams the stove door, too hard, stands up eyes blazing.

"How can you, my smart and so beautiful dear friend, stay one minute longer in that man's bed?"

"Marcel, he wants me to marry him."

But she knows her eyes are saying hold me. Marcel reads her look, takes a step closer, shrugs and turns away. He's tried that before. Their one kiss, weeks earlier, had opened for a moment to the piercing sweetness of love, before she whimpered and tore away.

So he answers gruffly, "Of course he does." His back to her, shrugging.

She slips the sandwiches to plates, he brings mugs of coffee, folds his spindly form into a chair. She curls in the cushions of his tattered couch. Instead of saying, "Listen, he says next month, he means it this time," she says, "Fair and I could move into town. We could take those rooms at Celeste's. She has a piano too."

Saying this and seeing how he glows, it actually takes shape, like a little round truth. Certainly she can leave Han and let herself fall in love with Marcel. The coffee is so strong she realizes in a pang that he used his precious drinking water supply for this. She can help him, yes, they'll make a cozy brave life together.

He dares to smile. "Would you?"

"I'll see what Fair says."

When the sun blazes briefly red just before it sets, she's walking her bike slowly up the other hill to the stately house that is her home now, lifting her eyes to its promise.

Electric lights are starting to go on in the windows and along the drive. Behind her in the darkening valley there is no electricity any more. Only a few solar generated lights for the lucky ones.

Wheeling her bike around to the side, she again catches sight of that little black shape against the far fence. Instead of calling for a Guard to dispel it once and for all, she sets off running towards it, boots spattering mud ridges.

The woman unmoving watches her. Face to face, Crea is the more disconcerted of the two. The huge dark eyes hold her astonished. In the tiny bent and bony body, those looming, furious eyes.

"Who are you?" Crea demands.

"I know who you are."

A tremulous sharp voice, French. Their frosted breaths meet.

"Why are you always standing here?"

"I am Fleur Chamois. You're living in my house."

Fleur's gray hair is awry under her black cap, but her shabby coat is elegantly cut. Mouth a folded down triangle amid a web of wrinkles. Crea hatless, coat open to the soft pink of her angora sweater, stares down at the audacious little bundle.

"This is Captain Hanley's house."

But Crea knows this is a lame defense. The house was requisitioned of course, like all the other spacious houses now occupied by important Guards and their families.

"They took it from us. Almost exactly five years ago today, February 2038, when my husband was sick. Tellement malade, tellement."

"Has he died then?"

"My Bernard. He died, yes. He was killed by that."

Crea goes limp against the fence.

"My husband died too," she murmurs.

Fleur ducks her head and her eyes come up luminous. "You loved him?"

Crea nods turning her face to the fence, pushing her forehead into the fragrant chill of freshly cut wood, pine from the forests dying so fast they can hardly use it quickly enough before it rots. Tears hot on cold cheeks. Fleur reaches up with a mittened hand to briefly touch them.

Crea turns. "I'm so sorry you lost your house."

"I've put a curse on it."

"What do you want me to do, I have a child."

"What you have to. But you'll never be happy there."

"Oh," Crea breathes, slumping with deep exhaustion, "I know that well enough. I don't expect that."

○

The American ambassador's wife is wearing blue silk with a red and white tiara. It's incredibly tacky, but somehow the effrontery works as defiance, which it's meant to do, because Tildy Mellon is a smart woman. The border has just been closed, only hours earlier. Her compatriots are now officially the beseechers they have already been for some years now. To enter Canada they either have to sneak across risking prison or even death, or possess elaborate papers proving their vital importance. At this very moment, the last miserable mass of American refugees is plodding through the town below. Of course, many of the resplendent guests around the dining tables in the glittering hall are Americans like Han who got here in time, a decade ago or more, and now share in the glory of power over desperate people.

Han at the head of the long host table in full uniform looks regal, on his lapels the gold braided sheaf of his rank, white hair cropped close to angular head, sharp benign eye on everything. Ambassador Mellon, in contrast, though a fit and handsome man, shrinks visibly. Lieutenant Renaud, when he's not checking Han for subtle cues, keeps his beefy face full on his gorgeous little vamp of a wife. He may close borders, but they say he can't keep track of Madame Renaud.

Crea in strapless white, a single strand of pearls at her neck, going through all the polite rituals, is amazed that others respond to her as a calm, charming woman when she's feeling frantic. From the other end of the table Han beams at her as always, continually calling attention to her with a nod or wink so nobody is likely to forget that this vision of female perfection is his.

The potage, a doubtless delicious blend of potatoes and leeks, leers up at her while she toys with it, throat closed. Boise Leonard, a plump brown-skinned man clever enough to have emigrated from Atlanta years ago, is regaling her with a banking story. She beams at him in gratitude. Boise's wife Ruella, splendid in lacey lavender, has just placed a red-nailed hand on Han's arm to emphasize a point. Han leans towards her appreciatively, turns his eyes to meet Crea's.

Before the thought even comes, Crea goes cold.

The pleasant hum of conversation continues amidst the clink of plates and forks. Waiters weave in and out, plates of venison arrive garlanded with pineapple, murmurs of admiration crest. Crea has to be persuaded to relinquish her soup spoon. She sits very still, freezing her gaze on Boise's chin. The odor of the meat nauseates her.

Han knows. Of course, how could she have been so idiotic as to believe she could hide Marcel from him, his loyal staff, his spies. Every single time she crept in the back door of that little shop to her secret license, he was told about it. And she had thought she had the freedom to choose!

She cuts the meat in small pieces and disperses it around her plate. Her skin feels intolerably hot, and the cold pearls that have taken on her heat burn her.

"So Canadian Mutual has a very good chance of coming out on top," Boise is boasting with his mouth full. "You wouldn't believe the odds, and it's not all luck, I can tell you, it's sheer nerve and verve."

She murmurs and nods, sips wine, wills her eyes away from Han. Relief, fear, mortification, defiance. At last one thought manages to form and hold: she can go now. She and Fair can pack up this very night and go to Marcel for good. She imagines him opening the door, his serious long face lit with joy, the magical kisses.

When the fish course comes, Crea is hungry. She devours the tangy trout while regaling Boise with an anecdote about Fair's music teacher.

On Boise's other side, Madame Renaud has tired of toying with the mayor, and now chimes in with a story of her own. It seems that her daughter, who wins equestrian prizes, was given a new horse for Christmas. She has named it Hector in honor of their esteemed leader. Isn't that wonderful?

Crea realizes that to her left Ambassador Mellon has been sitting in a silence almost as strained as her own, in spite of the valiant efforts of the kind little mayor's wife next to him.

"Are you staying at the Laurentian?" Crea asks him. "Do you find it comfortable?"

"Very comfortable," he intones. "Thank you."

What more can she say? Too bad your country is falling apart? Crea puts her napkin to her lips and lets herself look at Han. He and Ruella are listening incredulously to Tildy Mellon, who must be convincing them that she for one is not cowed. But when Han's eyes go to Crea, he beams and winks just as smug and possessive as before.

In the bathroom, Crea cools her cheeks and chest with cold water, touches up her hair, seeks comfort in the glowing reflection. What can he be thinking? What's he planning to do? Ignore it? Surely he will repudiate her now. He's only waiting for the most humiliating moment. Then, as she watches her beautiful face contort, she realizes that Marcel is in danger. Perhaps at this very moment he's opening that door not to the dream of Crea and Fair, but to Guards who seize him, drag him away. Of course they can fabricate charges against him, he's already suspect for lack of zeal. His arms are bound, his brave face bloodied.

Light in the library is so low that the books on the top shelves are shadows. Crea steps across the soft carpet to the glass doors. In March and April before it gets too hot these doors are kept open to the deck and garden. She cups her hands to see if she can catch a glimpse of Fleur.

Slowly she knows Han is already there, behind her, waiting. She turns. He's sitting in a high backed chair. He flips on the table lamp beside him.

"Darling," he says. "Taking a break? It's going well, I think, don't you?"

"Han…"

She starts the sentence, starts to step forward. But doesn't finish, doesn't step forward.

Words not spoken roil the air between them. The faraway sounds of their partying guests can't infer upon this wild silence. He watches her, fingertips tapping each other meditatively.

"I'm tired," she finally says.

"Of course. You really shouldn't have worked today. It's noble of you, but really, darling."

Crea makes a face that she hopes looks sheepish.

"We'll sleep in tomorrow," he says. His tone means sex.

He waits a moment, then gets up and moves to her. His hands are on her bare shoulders. His hands are cold. He presses her to him, reaching into her dress for her breasts. Just enough of an embrace to assert control.

"Now," he says, stepping back in satisfaction, "we must go and applaud the speeches."

"Han, please, don't."

"Why, my darling, whatever can you mean? Get hold of yourself and charm them all, as you do so well."

It's Ruella Leonard who gives the final toast. Her lovely cinnamon face is alight with excitement.

"And so, my friends, Canada is now safe. The hordes of bums and bandits have got to stay home. If it comes to war, so be it. With the help of our heroic Guards, we'll keep on building and protecting this great land of ours."

"Hear, hear!" "Vive le Canada!" "Go, Ruella!" "Victory!"

Ambassador Mellon goes so far as to touch his glass to his lips, but his wife Tildy stonily and rigidly glares. Her red white and blue looks even more garish against skin that has gone clammy white. As Crea numbly picks at the last of her blueberry mousse, she yearns to embrace Tildy, her suffering and her bravery. But she won't. She won't make any such gesture. And Tildy will continue to see only the gorgeous serene creature who pleasures the enemy.

Marguerite has drawn the drapes in the bedroom. The covers of the big plush bed are turned down in welcome. Han's brandy waits on the bedside table. It's almost midnight and the last sounds are fading into hush. Crea lifts one curtain. Stars are brilliant and the muddied grass has taken on an icy sheen. Of course Fleur would not be there now, but she's disappointed. She lets the curtain fall, unclasps her pearls. They lie warm in her palm.

Han is taking off his boots, jacket, shirt, looking at her looking at him. She feels her breath quicken. In a flash of self-loathing, she sees the extent of her complicity. She wants this world of luxury, security, indulgence, wants it for herself. She wants this sexual subservience, this man with a will of iron.

She places the pearls carefully in their box, slowly unzips her dress as Han comes to her, pushes her to her knees.

Episode 3

Distance

Crea at the age of twenty unwillingly finds herself in nursing school, and she can't seem to get the hang of bedside manners. When she's not sickened by the patients, she's crying over them. She hasn't yet, even after six months here, been able to put up that wall of emotional protection everyone tells her will soon be soothingly hers.

She looks up at the old man's face expecting a leer, sees only anxious gratitude. She's bathing him as he lies there with his ruddy bedsores, brown-spotted skin crumpled like crepe paper, the worn worm between his legs lifeless. Pity, and guilt at her revulsion, compel her to continue carefully washing his groin. Fascination too — she has never seen a penis that did not respond to her touch. George is seventy-eight and has not been out of bed for two years. Crea hopes she's at least doing this right.

"You'd be a terrific nurse," her mother Tati had said, lack of conviction betrayed in her too bright voice. "You're the most empathetic person I know, so gentle and caring."

"Not really. I hate wounded things, you know that. I could never even watch our dogs at the vet."

They were sitting at the kitchen table discussing Crea's options, a clouded sunset shafting greenish light across the floor. Shrugging off Tati's worried eagerness, Crea knew she was being unnecessarily sullen. But she was still crushed by the closing of her college in her sophomore year, so suddenly. One fall day in 2026 she was strolling around campus enjoying studying Mary Oliver, the next she was hugging friends for the last time and heading home. Many of her classmates from Concord High were back home too, as liberal arts colleges were closing right and left. The kids who had chosen vocational schools to start with were now envied.

So here she is, learning a trade.

"Thank you, miss," rasps the old man as Crea helps him back into his hospital garb. He has forgotten her name again, probably even her face. She smoothes the covers over him and smiles down, trying to stop imagining how he must be feeling. The only person who has ever come to visit him is a middle-aged granddaughter who lives in Indiana. George's immune system is a war zone.

"There now, you're all clean and all set," she says, trying to chirp cheerfully the way her superiors do. Especially the way Dr. Mellotti, formidable Dr. Mellotti, professor of geriatrics and dean of students at Mount Auburn Hospital, would want her to. The dean is tall and olive skinned, mid-forties, fierce beetle-browed face crunched around a thick nose, radiating an authoritarian charisma that sends students into shivers. Crea has never seen him smile. The benign paternal air he puts on for patients barely twitches at his thin lips even when he's being hearty. He has chastised Crea more than once for lack of poise. It is for him, for the approval he withholds no matter how hard she tries, that she is straining to succeed while at the same time convinced of her inadequacy.

At lunchtime she looks out the window at relentless February sleet and decides on the cafeteria, though she surely could use some fresh air. Passing through the walkway between buildings, she can see the Charles River swelling over its banks and over the roadway. Parading along in the water is the trash collected on its wayward journey, everything imaginable from plastic cups and condoms to tires and sticks of furniture, a perversely perky flotilla. Traffic is down to a few official trucks and buses sending up sheets of brown water like surfers. They say that so much rain this winter, plus rising seawater, means that the dam pumps between harbor and river have to work furiously day and night. Some people fear that fuel for the pumps is not a given, and if they cease to function, all east Cambridge as well as towns on the other side will be severely flooded. The hospital basement areas are already seeping wet.

Lined up in beds along the hallways lie the unfortunate patients for whom rooms have not yet been found. Bacteria immune to antibiotics, the comeback of old illnesses like polio, explosion of the whole gamut of cancers, and widespread outbreaks of new and old pulmonary diseases, are stretching the resources of all hospitals beyond their limits. Crea walks quickly, hates knowing the frightened eyes of the sick are following her. They would love a word from her, just a comforting word, a touch perhaps, but she can't do it. She's drained; she wants to lie down there herself.

Her roommates are in the cafeteria so Crea has to sit with them, even though two men trying to date her are at the same table and make room for her next to them. But she takes a chair on the other side, soothing them with a smile.

Nina sneers, "These boys are so hot for you, poor things. Look at the drools."

Nina is hawk faced with pimples, which makes her surly, but her caustic wit is fun when it's not aimed in your direction. She's also very smart and helps Crea with her homework. Crea shrugs good naturedly and tucks into her falafel salad, annoyed and embarrassed but playing the indulgent pal.

And of course Nina's right. The men have lost all interest in whatever conversation and are beaming all over Crea. She's used to it. She has known since ninth grade, when boys began flocking and male teachers gaping, that her beauty gives her power over men. Right now this certainty makes her tired. She parries their compliments and their hints at events they could accompany her to with a weariness that she fears comes across as sultry.

"How did the chem test go?" queries Nina.

"Not too bad. Thanks for your tips, they really helped."

"There's that movie about cloning in the Square," says the blond guy in her direction.

She smiles at him enigmatically without replying and gazes out over the packed cafeteria loud with voices, clinking dishes, scraping chairs.

"There's the Mellotti," she notes with a shudder.

"The atrocious Dr. M," groans Nina. "The face of a monkey Dr. M."

"Who's he honoring with his presence?" says the blond. "Oh yeah, he's sitting with that suck-up Todd."

"He's married," says Crea.

"Who, M or Todd?"

"Both," says Nina. "M's wife's an MD too."

"Todd's is a movie star," grins the blond. "A knockout."

Nina says, "M's is even uglier than he is."

"What a coupling!" guffaws the blond.

Everybody laughs, but Crea's heart sinks. She's very much afraid that if this last chemistry exam doesn't turn out to be a big improvement, grim Dr. M will call her in for another dressing down. These interviews have come to be confusing as well as frightening for Crea, because as he scolds he puts his face so close to hers she can smell his breath and hair. That someone with such godlike authority and severity would even have a smell is in itself disconcerting. Nothing she says ever seems to satisfy him, no matter how hard she tries.

Sure enough, when she gets back to her dorm that evening, she finds a notice from the dean's office. She's summoned there tomorrow at ten.

○

Tati leaves work in Boston and runs for the bus, looking forward to her evening alone, the freedom to think about Jake at leisure.

Martin's constant presence is a weight, and tonight is his teaching night. He doesn't talk much, but when he does, she's expected to partake. He retired three years ago when Tufts University had to close, but he was on the way out anyway. They had actually been in the process of offering him a disability pension for his depression. Just recently he has started teaching contemporary poetry one night a week at an adult education center, and he actually likes it. Tati dares to hope it will cheer him up.

She herself doesn't like her job as salesperson at Staples, though she knows she's lucky to have one. She misses the bustle and challenge of the architecture firm, where her talents came into play every hour. In those days when she came home from work, she was sapped as after a race, ex-hilarated, surfeited. Now she comes home in an exhaustion of frustration and boredom.

It's a watery evening, drizzle tapering off into a colorless sunset, anemic and tremulous. Tati is relieved to turn into her quiet street off the main thoroughfare, away from the homeless people huddled in doorways — the rain made them dismantle their makeshift abodes of cardboard and debris. The smog is weaker here in Concord and she slows to inhale sharp earthy air, noting new shoots of green thrusting up in her neighbors' front yards.

Today Jake kissed her hand again. He works in the computer department, a pudgy bearded man with deep blue eyes, about fifty, her age. Whenever she goes into the stockroom he follows her, no longer giving excuses, just smiling and telling her how much he likes her. And lately he has escalated to taking her hand and holding it to his lips. She enjoys this wildly, though she sees how ridiculous it is.

"We should have lunch alone together," he often says.

She always laughs. "It would look funny now, wouldn't it? Everybody here has lunch in the same place. People would get ideas."

He munches at her palm and murmurs, "I have ideas," sparkling his eyes at her.

The heat of his mouth and hand are titillating but she just shrugs and tosses at him, "Oh Jake don't be silly. We're both married."

"But we like each other," he mischievously reasons.

When she gets back to her counter she's breathing a little fast and she's warm.

So far this is cute and fun, she reflects turning into her gate, but she'll have to watch it. Probably he doesn't mean a word of it, but also maybe he does. There's no way she wants to get into a mess with Jake.

The house greets her with her love for it. They've lived here in this pretty yellow clapboard house in Concord for twelve years now, since the days when they were still happy. Colors burnt orange and rose, grand paintings, tall shelves of books, comfort, brightness, crisp frilly curtains in the kitchen. On the fridge a snapshot of Crea and Martin at Christmas, Crea luminous beside her drooping gray father like sun in clouds.

Outside the back window the grand old wet-black maple splaying its magnificent naked limbs against lead sky, snowdrops blooming already in the spongy grass. Last birds dash by in bedtime rituals. As Tati cooks and twilight closes down, sleet begins again.

The television news is the usual mix of trivial dramas sprinkled with brief allusions to ominous facts. Tati is able to glean that another reservoir has closed, something about solvents, metals, pesticides, radioactive waste. "Once these long-lived pollutants make their way into the underground water supply," intones the doleful man being interviewed, "the damage is virtually irreversible." He especially laments chemical compounds that act like the hormones controlling reproduction, "the estrogen mimics driving amphibians to extinction." But when he starts to talk about their effect on humans, the reporter cuts him off and jumps with gusto into a long story about a movie star's divorce.

Tati is in her pajamas curled up on the couch with a book when it occurs to her that the news tonight did not mention the election. It was supposed to have taken place last November, but was postponed until May. The presidential candidates had seemed to agree that this was a good idea. Every once in a while one of them gives an impassioned speech, but less and less often do commentators bother to cover them. Tati drops the book to her lap and stares into space at an appalling idea. Suppose they never have another election? They could just go on postponing it until everybody gets tired and drops the subject. In the pit of her stomach she feels as if she's just witnessed a murder. She grew up with regular elections, traditional campaigns, reassuring congratulations and reconciliations among candidates once one of them won.

She reasons with herself. It's true that the national debt is so atrocious that all social services, even social security, have had to be privatized to save the country from bankruptcy. And now that they're privately owned, they're being shredded by the fluctuations of the depressed market. The President was elected precisely because he's also the CEO of the largest American corporation, with the obvious know-how needed in such a financial crisis. Surely, when the upheavals caused by current extreme weather events are under control, the election will duly take place. People will insist.

But Tati can't subdue her gnawing feeling, and not for the first time, that something bizarre and terrifying has been unleashed. The country is besieged from every direction, in terrible shape on every front, yet people don't seem to want to talk about it. There's an undercurrent of hysteria that grows the more it's suppressed, the more the surface pretense of normality gleams artificial. She finds that the topic alienates her friends when she brings it up, as if she's purposefully spoiling their day. At the same time, many of them seem more tense, more impetuous, careless about things they once prized.

She's sitting there staring at her thoughts when she hears Martin's key, his briefcase hitting the floor, his heavy tread.

She calls, "Hi. There's casserole left over if you want it."

She doesn't expect him to answer. Martin hoards his words like treasure. So she's surprised when he comes into the living room with a jolly greeting. Now she realizes how late he is, it's almost eleven.

"Students took me out for a beer," he says proudly, in the exact same tone a boy would announce he made the football team.

Tati responds happily. "Great!" She knows how hard it is for him nowadays to socialize and relate to people.

He sits down next to her on the couch. She tentatively experiments with leaning against him. Feeling him, the old beloved weight, she realizes that what she wants most in the world is for him to kiss her. Truly and deeply kiss her, like he used to. His face is flushed as he smiles and tells her about the students and the class. It's wonderful that he's talking to her, that he's here. If this is a sign of things to come, her heart might yet smile again. He puts his arm around her and goes to sleep. She sits there for a long time, listening to his peaceful snore, memorizing the warmth.

○

"It's not only your grades," snaps Dr. Mellotti. "You know very well, as I have often told you, that your way of relating to patients is too personal."

Crea sits up straight in her chair across from his desk, trying to look contrite and absorbed. But in truth she feels destroyed. How can she ever hope to measure up? When he told her that she got a C on her chem test, she waited happily for his praise. But he seems as angry as ever. She's been here for twenty minutes, she has a class in half an hour. He gets up and comes around the desk, pulls up a chair close to hers.

"What do you have to say for yourself?" he asks. "Young lady."

She tries to smile. "I think I'm improving, doctor."

"I really care about your success, my dear," he goes on, inching the chair up so his knees brush hers. His face is close and his dark eyes exaggerated by glasses swim over her. "I want to help you, now you know that's true."

Crea's emotions — confusion, amusement, annoyance, anxiety — crystallize in a set of seconds during which she wonders if Dr. M is coming on to her, rejects the idea as ludicrous, and accepts it with dawning horror. Now all the signals come clear. He's leering. His knees press in, the heat of his breath is not anger. In fact, Dr. M is beside himself with lust — she has seen the symptoms a hundred times in the young men who pursue her. But no, surely not this man old enough to be her father, this husband of someone, this icon, this master of her fate! She's frozen.

Dr. M seems to be interpreting her paralysis as some kind of acquiescence. His spidery hands with their hairy knuckles are dabbing at her skirt. She suddenly worries that the cloth of her crisp pale blue uniform is too tight across her breasts, her white-stockinged legs too exposed.

"Crea, my dear, you do feel it too, don't you? Say you do, come on. Be kind, be good. I can't stand it."

"I have a class," she whispers inanely.

"Of course you do, my angel, of course you do."

His palms are flat on her thighs now, moving. She puts her hands on them and pushes him back.

"It's at eleven," she says more strongly. "Post-op Procedures."

She stands up. He grabs her around the waist and pushes his face into her stomach.

"Oh please," he mutters. "Just stay a little longer."

His voice is strange, strangled. She looks out over the spacious room, desk, computer set, filing cabinets, leathery chairs, substantial proof of his authority, feels the press of his head and arms. So it's meaningless that her studies have improved. She'd stupidly thought that her hard work would bring Dr. M's appreciation and admiration, when in fact his attentions had nothing to do with her brain at all. She feels her old passive capitulation to the fate of her attraction, and at the same time the compensating thrill of sexual power. The tables have turned entirely, the master now the supplicant. She slowly sits down again. While he kisses her she doesn't move.

The next evening Crea is waiting for Dr. Mellotti on a small street off Mt. Auburn. Sounds of rush hour traffic are dulled in this little enclave of affluent colonial-style houses with their low white fences and lushly draped windows. She stays in the shadows, a nervous accomplice, tensely aware that they must not be seen. Not just because he has a wife, not just because any observer could guess in an instant what they are up to, but because her friends would never stop torturing her with jokes about it. The thrill of power she feels is offset by fear of ridicule, or worse, envy. His car pulls up and she crosses the street to get in quickly.

They have dinner in a tiny French restaurant in the South End. Dr. M steers her masterfully past the heaps of homeless crouching in the sooty mist, down a narrow brick sidewalk where in the gloom the bright doorway suddenly springs up gaily. He gives a false name and they are seated in a dim corner, with one candle.

So this is what it's like to date a famous doctor! Crea is beginning to enjoy the adventure. The boys she has known fade before the stature and influence of this brilliant mature man. She's wearing a delicate demure blouse that she knows excites him. It's silky pale pink, with frills adorning the transparent sleeves and low neck, a little loose bow instead of buttons. When she leans forward he can just glimpse the rounding of her breasts.

They drink exquisite wine and talk about Crea. He listens kindly and intently to her childhood stories, her regrets and dreams. She decides he's not so ugly after all. His swarthy face glows with devotion. His shoulders are square and purposeful. His sinewy hands are expressive, long-fingered, elegant. She remembers them on her thighs. She's just realizing that she would like him to kiss her again, when he says, "I know a little motel, okay?"

She pauses with a forkful of chocolate mousse. Has he read her mind? She's embarrassed, looks away. The few other occupied tables hold couples just as intent upon each other, clearly not listening to this conversation

that suddenly makes her blush. A motel. She hadn't thought of that. She's
better acquainted with the back seats of cars and bunk beds. Well, what
had she expected? She takes a searing swallow of brandy.

"What about your wife?"

"She's not well," he says shortly.

Crea puts down her glass, startled. "What's the matter with her?"

This is an obstacle she hadn't foreseen. She had decided that Mrs. M's
harried and ambitious medical career caused her to terribly neglect poor
Dr. M. Now she'll have to revise the tale she has spun, her own role as
heroine.

"Emphysema," he says. "She has to be on oxygen all the time. Even
walking around she has to be hooked up to a machine all the time." He
urges, agitated, "Don't you see what this means? She can't ever get out of
breath. She can't ever make love."

"Well, but, then maybe she doesn't mind if…"

"I don't know. I'm not going to ask her, if that's what you mean. But
why should she mind? I mean, I'm human."

Crea is a bit dazed processing this new information, but she says, "I
don't suppose I blame you. After all…"

"I'm a man, I'm a man, Crea." His voice is so gentle. "And I adore
you."

The motel, like the restaurant, is tucked away discretely, somewhere off
the highway. But the room is lovely with muted light, plush carpet, vast
quilted bed. He begs her to call him baby.

◯

Tati's boss is in a foul mood. The roads from Pennsylvania are flooded
again, so shipments are late again, and gas prices have doubled again. The
products will hardly sell at cost when they do arrive. He gruffly orders Tati
to check inventory and she heads for the stockroom happy to be off the
floor, anticipating Jake. But though she stays as long as feasible, he doesn't
show up, and she returns to her counter disappointed, the world drab
again. At lunchtime she sits in a booth with three other women, gossiping
about a pregnant colleague and fretting that more people may soon be laid
off. She watches Jake eating on the other side of the room, admires the
solid set of his shoulders. His hair is graying but his beard is Viking blond.
He meets her eyes from time to time with a mischievous squint.

Her heart lightens with the fun of it and she's reminded of the summer
when Crea was two, still cherubic with baby fat, obsessed with the word
"No." For two weeks in August they rented a cottage near the beach. She
and Martin became kids again with Crea, running circles in the sand,
splashing each other in the waves, building sand castles, marveling at peculiar shells, staring into mysterious tidal pools. While Crea napped, their

play turned to sex, not just making love but poking and tickling, giggling and whispering, sticking out their tongues, lapping in odd places like puppies, being naughty. Somehow, connecting with their child in that wild beautiful place liberated them from adulthood. One afternoon, while Crea just waking from her nap in the other room was gaily practicing "No" in every decibel, Martin and Tati were rolling naked on the sandy ratty rug, faint with laughter, chanting "yes, yes, yes!"

She gives Jake a smile so wide and free that it feels like she's got her face back again.

That afternoon she and Jake are alone only once in the stockroom, between high shelves of packages and equipment. He massages her hand in both of his and takes it to his mouth. His beard and moustache are soft on her palm, her wrist. He moistens her fingertips and she closes her eyes. They don't say anything.

After dinner, Tati says to Martin, "I was wondering."

He doesn't answer, piling dishes into the sink, running water over them, leaving them for her to finish. She asks him if he heard her. Without turning around he goes off into the living room to watch something on TV, anything, he doesn't really seem to care what it is. Tonight it's a comedy about colonizing the moon. Standing behind his chair, addressing the back of his balding head, Tati continues talking.

"I was wondering if you'd like to make love. We haven't made love for almost a year now. I was wondering if you're feeling better and could manage it."

The TV screen flashes the naked torso of a voluptuous young woman with blue skin who it seems is a robot.

Tati pursues, "You see, I don't think I'm ready to stop having sex. I'm too young, really I am, though you always talk about how old we are now. We're not. I'm still pretty cute, Martin, haven't you noticed? Other men notice. So I was wondering…"

She stops. She almost envies him his dogged absorption in the flickering artifice before him. If she could join him in his dead world, she would.

She goes upstairs and gets into bed and pleasures herself. She conjures up Jake, imagining him naked; she thinks about the eager fawn-eyed grad student she bedded all that crazy summer five years ago. But she lingers most of all on Martin coming to her the way he was that time at the beach, his hungry tongue, his strong young legs. The intensity of her orgasm, in spite of the relief, deeply saddens her. Not just that Martin isn't there, but that he doesn't want to be.

○

Mt. Auburn Hospital's new pulmonary wing opens with fanfare. The dedication ceremony, which has drawn many dignitaries including the governor, takes place appropriately during the first heat wave of the year, in mid April. Smog has thickened and the air is heavy. Warnings have gone out to avoid unnecessary outdoor exercise. Crea decides to wear a light flowered dress with only a suggestion of sleeves, and a pink straw hat with a floppy brim. Under the hat's shadow her bright hair curls loose over her shoulders.

She and Nina walk together from the dorm. Late afternoon sun glitters the still swollen river, glances off in blinding shafts. There's a clutch of cars and TV cameras at the new wing's entrance.

"You know, I'm sure," comments Nina with a sharp sidelong glance, "Mrs. Dr. M is giving the keynote."

"That's to be expected, she's got lung problems herself."

"Have you ever seen her?"

"Nope."

Nina pursues with a malicious tang, "Don't pretend you're not interested. The way Dr. M looks at you."

Crea shrugs. "I guess." Nina is too smart, she just might get a clue. "I can't help it, for God's sake, poor monster man."

Nina laughs. "Poor gorgeous girl. What's it like, fighting off men all the time?"

"No fun, believe me. I'd rather concentrate on the important things in life, like passing finals."

"Which you will do." And she clearly can't help adding, "Especially old M's course. You've been doing really well in that."

They sit with other students toward the back of the crowd. Crea is suddenly thirsty and realizes that her mouth is dry from nervous anticipation. She very much both does and doesn't want to see what his wife is like. She gets a young man to go find water for her. He returns after a long time and hands her a cup proudly.

"I had to go the hell all the way over to…" he is boasting, swaggering at her.

Crea thanks him vaguely, her eyes glued to the stage. There she is, that must be Mrs. M, a thickset dark-haired woman toting what looks like a black golf bag, from which creeps a long plastic twine attached to her nostrils. She's out of breath and gasping as she's led to her seat near the podium. She sits there fighting for air, frighteningly fragile.

Voices drone over the loud speaker but Crea's mind is in the motel room, Dr. M's body pressing at her, his mouth burning her breasts, his pitiable beseeching moans. They go there almost every week now, often in the afternoon. Seldom do they any longer bother with dinner. It has become a driving secret ritual that Crea can't ever seem to question. She's drunk with her dual role as conniving and innocent, helpless and all-powerful. She refuses to acknowledge the fear that her dominion is only fleeting, that one day the mighty doctor will thunder rejection and condemnation.

Mrs. M stands up slowly. She's breathing normally now, and her voice is rich and soft. She talks about the children the new wing will serve, "who otherwise would not have a chance at a normal life," about new equipment, generous donors, hopes for cures and cleaner air. She may have once been pretty. Her eyes have a coy slant, her little red mouth smiles gravely. She has children, Dr. M's children, teenagers now. She lives with him in his house, he goes home to her every night, they bring up their kids together. This information dawns on Crea as if new. She starts to feel very strange, as if she's not awake, or just waking.

Afterwards, as they all get up and head for the reception, the man next to her queries, "Are you all right? You look kind of faint."

Nina studies her with too much interest.

"It's just the heat," Crea tells them.

She gulps the wine someone hands her, stuffs her mouth with sour cream dip. She talks gaily and nervously with her friends, watching Dr. M and his wife, who are standing together chatting with the governor acknowledging the deferent attention of attendees. A chair is brought for Mrs. M, and her husband fusses over getting her seated comfortably, rests his hand on her shoulder.

Crea works her way around behind them, sidles up near enough to note that Mrs. M's black hair is well cut and probably dyed, her hands are small and freckled, her wedding ring is accompanied by a large diamond. At the back of her neck rolls the frilled collar of her white blouse. Next to it serenely lies Dr. M's hand, which Crea knows so well.

Without thinking, with an urge mindless and physical, Crea moves around to stand in front of them. She pretends to be fascinated by the governor, noting that Dr. M is frozen with fear, and Mrs. M totally clueless. Crea is enjoying the moment asserting and displaying herself, but at the same time suffering intensely from jealousy and shame. Mrs. M smiles up wanly at the young blond girl under the pink hat, offering her hand. Crea takes it and keeps it too long, its cool dampness, the smell of perfume and antiseptic. She wants to fall at the woman's feet in sobs of confession, wants to slap her, wants to scream with laughter. She meets Dr. M's alarmed eyes with a slow shake of her head.

○

On Saturday, Crea takes the commuter train out to Concord. She doesn't tell her parents she's coming. It would involve some sort of explanation, which she doesn't feel up to fabricating. The heat has subsided and it's a beautiful afternoon, airy golden like spring should be. She walks down the familiar streets greeting people she's known since childhood. Already she feels nurtured.

She lets herself in the back door, automatically goes to the fridge, pours a glass of milk, finds cookies where they always are.

"Anybody home?" she calls.

There's no answer, but she knows that doesn't preclude her father being somewhere around. She checks the rooms and finds him asleep on the sofa in his study. Not surprised, she shrugs sadly, decides for now not to wake him. Her bedroom is unchanged, except of course it's far cleaner than it ever was when she lived there. She ponders her rock star posters, frayed teddy bear, silly scribbles on the wall. She feels alien in this teenage world.

While Crea is flipping through her high school yearbook in disbelief, Tati is on her favorite run, jogging along the trail that follows the Assabet River. Because of the air alerts, it's been weeks since she did anything more strenuous than dash for the bus, and she feels her rusty body respond first with reluctance, then gratitude. She breaks through to her second wind on the way down a curving slope, smiling into the rushing air, floating on her acquiescent muscles. On her left the woods with shiny yellowish newborn leaves curling out like welcoming hands, on her right across the river the fields mellow rolling out of winter's pall. At one point she stops to rest, stretching her legs leaning against a tree, looking down the bluff at the river dancing on its way, thinking of the creatures inside its world, from fish to frogs to worms, doing their living with much the same intent and frustration and satisfaction as she's doing hers.

By the time Tati reaches home, her pounding heart is light. She finds Crea in the study talking to Martin.

Delighted, she backs off. "Don't hug me, I'm dripping, wait til I shower."

While her mother's upstairs, Crea tries again.

"What I'm saying, dad, is not that you're a bad person or any such thing. I just want to see you get more out of life. You just sit around here all day."

Her father slumped on the sofa shakes his head. "You're criticizing me again."

"No, dad, I'm not!"

"Then leave me alone, why don't you? I have work to do."

Of course she wants to reply, "What work?" but this is his old standby pretense and she's tired of hurting his feelings — she's not getting anywhere.

"Sure, dad. Hey do you want to hear about my patients…or would you rather wait til later?"

Martin gets up and lumbers over to sit at his desk, switches on his computer busily. Crea turns away, the old aching acid loss of him, the ghost of him, wrenching up to her throat. She barely remembers the man he was when she was his little princess, but she does recall how it made her feel and she mourns that feeling.

She's out wandering around in the garden when Tati appears, bearing a bowl of chips and glasses of lemonade. She looks good, Crea thinks; the gray slashes through her auburn hair are dramatic, her shorts show shapely legs. Of course she's gained weight in recent years, hormones diminishing no doubt, but she still has that air of adventure and verve. They sit at the table on the patio looking out over the mud brown yard spiked with green, the umbrella shading them, as they have so often in the past that for both of them it's a communication in itself.

While they talk about her schoolwork, Crea wonders if she'll be able to say anything at all to her mother about Dr. M. She desperately needs to, but the old barriers and resentments strain through. She doesn't quite trust that she won't be judged, made to feel small and bad.

She tries, "The dean is a strict old guy. He made me shape up."

Tati has not caught her tone. "Kudos to him."

"He's in his forties, forty-five I think. His wife has emphysema."

"A terrible disease. There's so much of it these days. Good thing they've built that new wing at your hospital. But what we desperately need is some real action in the political arena. This stuff they're doing, like rationing gas, Sunday afternoon brownouts, phasing out pesticides, banning incinerators, taxing plastics, and making such a drama about it, it's all too little too late. They've got to do something really drastic now, but I don't see any sign of it."

Crea doesn't want to talk politics. She's annoyed by her mother's constant reminder that in her own childhood the climate used to be normal. She tends to read Tati's tirades on global warming as some kind of superiority trip. Even so, she's now beginning to realize the frightening truth, and actually envies Tati having known the seasons when they were whole and balanced.

She surprises herself by saying, "I'd like to hear more about it, mom. What summer and winter used to be like."

Tati turns to look fully at her, alerted for the first time to some edge in her daughter's manner. This willingness to hear more about a subject she has always barely tolerated is in a way just another signpost on the journey of growing up. But aside from Tati's gratification about this specific opening, she senses a deeper alteration. Perhaps Crea came home today for a particular reason.

"That's great, dear," Tati grins. "Now tell me more about your courses, your roommates, this mean Dr. M. How is that poor old man George?

How's Nina? How's your love life? Any nice guys in the picture?"

At the end of a deep breath, Crea says, "I've got a problem, mom. I hope you don't get all worked up over it. This doctor…"

Tati knows the whole story before Crea says anything more. As the afternoon sun drops behind the maple tree, Tati watches her daughter telling the ancient tale of older married man and young female admirer as if it happened to the world for the first time. She frets again over her daughter's incredible beauty, at her naiveté, her penchant for dependent devotion — what a dangerous mix! Crea has the looks of a Botticelli Venus, and none of the tough armor she needs to counter the effect. While Tati has sometimes found herself in jealous awe of Crea's power over men, she has also always felt remiss in not giving her more ammunition to counter the consequences.

Now Crea is crying and Tati is holding her.

"I never want to see him again, I don't know what to do!"

"Poor baby, it's okay. It's going to be okay."

Tati lets her mother's milk of solace flow, fleeting back to the long ago sobbing child in her arms memorialized, lulled in the trance of it, the wholeness. As she holds her daughter, as she receives and swallows each sob into herself, taking on the pain and making it hers, Tati subsumes the whole of Crea's life and all her own motherhood in a surge. The screaming infant, the tantrum toddler, frustrated wails, angry shouts, arms around her neck, precious pressure, love deeper than unfathomable.

Crea clinging to her mother, knowing her peaceful smell, accepting her old helpless donation, briefly trusts. But she pulls away the more abruptly. She's hiccupping, apologizing, blowing her nose, smiling sheepishly, sitting back down in the chair, sipping last lemonade. The moment is over but the exchange has been made: mother's heart is heavier and child's lighter.

"Thanks, mom, I feel better."

In the silence while they sit together again watching sky colors shift in pale orange tones, clouds quickening in a sudden wind, Tati knows she should give advice, but hardly knows what. She's furious with this lecherous doctor who took advantage of his status, and annoyed by Crea's blind girlish romanticism, but her own close acquaintance with lust melts her indignation. Instead of judgment she feels kinship with her daughter. Perhaps as much as Jake, Dr. M is a response to Martin, who left them both in the lurch, his glowing promise as husband and father betrayed. Martin's depression seduced him away, and like a jealous mistress has allowed him only fleeting symbolic relationships with his family. Wife and child have been compelled to search for him in other men.

Clouds are now racing past changing shape rapidly like cartoon spies switching disguises, one second a serpent, another a tower, then a jumble of wrestling forms, then jagged slashes. The storm grabs the umbrella above them in a violent embrace and turns it inside out.

The women laugh together, their laughter seized by the wind, intertwined, dashed away. As they hurry to gather up the dishes, hair wilding, clothes flapping, the sky suddenly falls dark gray as if eyes have closed over it. Rain will come any minute, hard and vicious, no nurture in its drive at the earth already soaked to exhaustion.

Episode 4

Touch and Go

It's April in Vermont. The refugee camp just outside Burlington simmers in grueling noontime heat. Scores of people are laboring through it, to construct a stage for Zoria in time for the great guru's visit. She's coming here to perform an Easter celebration this very Sunday.

Zoria has been pregnant with Jesus for three years now, since her divine visitation in 2040. Over and over her gospel is being broadcast on loudspeakers throughout the camp, interspersed with popular religious and patriotic tunes. She says his Second Coming will occur when we've all truly regretted our sins and bowed down in humility and gratitude to her.

"God has promised!" Zoria's throaty wheeze claws the sodden air. The blue sky that seems to be bringing her voice is a startling blaze. "As soon as the people have cast aside their rebellious ways to embrace your Zoria, Earth will be made whole, air and water cleansed, mutations reversed, the seasons restored, and Jesus will walk among us again!"

It seems that all you have to do is believe in Zoria, build her a temple, and give her your money.

"What a lot of crap," mutters Leon.

He bites viciously into his sandwich. He and Tati are sitting with a dozen others in the shade under the scaffolding. Even so, sunlight manages to slip through the planks, each slice of it burning. The sound of hammering continues around them.

"How wonderful to be able to believe that," she says, "to believe it's not hopeless."

"It's not hopeless up in Newfoundland. We just have to get there."

"Same planet, only a lot farther north. It's happening there too."

Others chime in. Just having this argument animates them, gives them the vision of a bearable future. Several people take issue with Leon's disparagement of the guru.

"I'm betting on Zoria. What she says is true. Just look around, like she says."

"She makes things happen. She said fifty thousand people would die of cholera and they did, didn't they? See. And she told us about the tidal waves over Boston way beforehand. She's close with God, I'm telling you."

Someone snorts at Leon, "Jesus won't choose you when he comes back. You'll be sorry."

Tati no longer wants to scream at them. She only comments mildly, "God didn't do this to the world, we did."

Leon agrees, "You can't think God wanted Creation defiled," but is drowned out with choruses of "Zoria says…"

Time to get back to work. He takes a last sip from Tati's canteen. She urges more on him, but they both know she needs it for the trip into town.

Against his will and against his conscience, Leon has to work on the stage.
They need the food.

His lips on hers are dry. She turns once to wave again. His stooped
shoulders in shirtless overalls, under the wide hat his grim old precious
face.

Tati passes between tents strung with clotheslines twirling kaleido-
scopes of shapes and colors, a gigantic soup caldron standing steamy sentry
by the kitchen tent, the picturesque little white church that serves as medical center. Her angular stride, gray hair tucked up into broad hat, smiling
here and there greeting an acquaintance or a child.

In its center the camp is laid out in mathematically precise lines of
huge tents along paths. But beyond this inner circle, government efficiency long since abandoned, bunches of small tents are pitched haphazardly.
And finally, near the trench latrines crouch a dozen makeshift shelters,
crafted with old tires, rugs, metal rods, ragged plastic sheeting. One family
has domesticated a school bus — without wheels, jaunty yellow chipped,
in the doorway a gaunt woman holding a baby. Tati smiles at them but the
stink of the latrines clutches her throat and hurries her past.

The road to the highway is soft dust. Smells begin to clear and sweeten.
A cluster of apple trees billows pink-white, bees visiting them. She goes to
look.

Wings whirr plump striped bodies diving, burrowing, beveling into
flower meat. Watching, after a while she begins to wonder if all the bees
know what they're doing. Aren't they supposed to fix on the bloom center
and zoom straight in? Instead, some of them seem to be wandering, bumping into petals, confused. Tati can't remember how many summers it's been
since she saw bees. She and Leon have only been in Vermont since they
ran out of fuel in November. She keeps on standing there in the mauve
shade that's shifting patterns in a small breeze, dreamed by the sensual
ritual and urgent omm sound, pollen and honey.

Smiling at her turbulent brain's acquiescence to this sensory delight,
she remembers Greg. For pure escape, nothing has ever matched Greg.
She thinks of him as a boy even though he was nearly thirty then. He
was so bony and pale, with the open rosy-mouthed face of a Renaissance
innocent, the mop of curly fawn colored hair. She was forty-five and going through the daily stress of her husband's depression, plus her teenage
daughter's discovery of alcohol and boys. Tati escaped to Greg's little
apartment when she could, for afternoons of mindless passion. He played
Edith Piaf while they sweated on his narrow bed. To this day she can never
hear Piaf without replaying the thrust of him, his strange mewing cries, his
ecstatic baby face.

"Phytoplankton," he would say, "are the mainstay of life on Earth."

He was writing his graduate thesis on ocean food chains.

"Listen to what these little critters do." Stroking her flushed thigh, thumbing her nipples or lips. "These tiny phytos, these one-celled plants, they absorb carbon dioxide and give back half of all our oxygen! Not only that, they're the base of the food chain, the zooplankton eat them and even whales eat zooplankton."

Tati listened dreamily, taking it as story. But she knew how serious he was. By that time, in the early 2020s, the oceans were in serious trouble. Cod and tuna were already extinct, the Gulf Stream had slowed, cyclones and tidal waves were tripling in strength and frequency. Now, twenty years later, she wonders why everyone didn't run out into the streets screaming, "Stop!" Well, they had problems of their own. They went about their business.

She heard about Greg's suicide many years after it happened. Drowned himself, they said. How? She sees him swimming white naked into the horizon.

The highway is busy with bicycles, here and there a horse and wagon, an ancient car. Whoosh, clop, clank in the boiling sun. The only post office in Burlington with eview access is in the middle of town. Along the gray brick street striated with weeds many of the shops are closed and boarded up. To her left down the slopes she can glimpse Lake Champlain, shimmering blue. To her right the forested green but browning mountains, tops pricked with lazily twirling white wind turbines. There's a long line for the eview cubicles, but that's to be expected, and she's early anyway. Her arrangement with Crea is for two o'clock.

The last time she talked to her daughter was two months ago, soon after the border was closed. The exchange became terse, Crea insisting her future husband could guarantee passage to Canada only for Tati, and Tati maintaining she would not leave without Leon. Crea was near tears. "How can you miss my wedding?!" She didn't look well, or maybe it was just the poor reception that day. Only two years since Crea's first husband died quickly of cholera, and now she's getting married again to some middle-aged military man, Tati had fretted, while managing to say, "I'm so happy for you." Since then she had vowed a hundred times to be more accepting of her daughter's new life, proffer more affection and support.

At last it's her turn. The man ahead of her comes out of the cubicle sobbing, from whatever his own devastating news. She presses in the code for which she has paid an exorbitant price, waits while the picture swims into view. And there is Crea. Her child.

"Mom, mom, it's so good to see you! How are you? Are you okay?"

Crea is so beautiful. Hair still as silvery blond as in childhood, longer now and curling loose around her shoulders, large black-lashed eyes glowing earth brown. She's looking poised and professional, dark tailored jacket over elegant blouse. Of course, she's in her office at the newspaper, but still Tati is awed. She hungrily drinks in the sight of her, for a few seconds tasting joy. They chat happily about Fair, now eleven. Yes, she's still crazy about music, is taking horseback riding. Sure, she's healthy, she's fine. But then, of course, it starts.

"Han says he can get you in if you just go up to the border right across from St. Jean. Ask for Lieutenant Caron."

"Sweetheart, no. I'm not leaving Leon. We'll have to wait until he can come too."

"What do you mean? Why is this Leon person so important? How can you care about him more than Fair and me?"

Crea hears her voice rising, stops, studies her mother. So old, she looks so old. Wasn't it only yesterday mom's hair was the color of wheat, her skin smooth?

"Okay, okay." Crea takes a patient breath. "You love him?"

"I guess I do. Yes." Tati's sudden smile is like the old days, beaming her whole face. "Just can't help it." Then she pleads, "Please try to understand. Remember he insisted on staying with me til your grandfather died. He could have left much earlier, probably in time to get across the border before it closed. He's been so loyal, protective, I don't know how I ... ," she ends with a shrug of appeal.

Tati is wearing a sleeveless dress a bit too small, starting to fray. Crea reluctantly recognizes how poor they must be. As deprived perhaps as the pitiful mass of American refugees until recently threading past her splendid house in Petit Chapeau. Now the border is closed, so they don't haunt her as vividly. But she certainly doesn't want to dwell on the idea her mother is one of them.

Tati twists her hands together, begins tentatively, "When do you think…do you think Han will be able to get papers for Leon too?"

Her mother's humility, so out of character, cracks Crea's resentment over Leon, opens her heart out. She has come to understand Tati as a woman, passionate, and strong. Tati will not like Han.

"Of course he'll get them," Crea assures her. "It's already in the works. He's guessing sometime this summer."

"Summer."

For Tati the word hurts. Already the heat stabs so cruelly. How will they endure a summer in these tents?

Crea reads her grimace as remonstrance.

"Mom, he's doing his best," she says sharply. "You know you could come today if you wanted to."

"Yes, yes, of course. Thank him for me, for us. Tell him how sorry I am to have missed the wedding."

"It was picture perfect. Fair was dressed all in pink ruffles and carried my train. We wove a garland of rosebuds in her hair."

Guiltily, Crea knows that any mention of Fair sharpens her mother's longing to come. She also knows she's basically lying in not conveying her ambivalence about Han. How comforting it would be to tell her everything!

Tati's shining moment picturing Fair is darkened by thinking, rosebuds! A train! How affluent is this captain of hers? What kind of world? She stares at her daughter as from a cosmic distance.

Crea says, "You'll be here by Fair's next birthday for sure. Don't worry."

Soon it's time for goodbye. Tati has paid for twenty minutes, and more people are waiting their turn before the four o'clock brownout.

In the street she lingers in the shade of the building, savoring the lake. She knows that if she gets much closer she'll see half a mile of baked exposed lakebed left by years of receding water, so she keeps her distance. A breeze has come up, frothing little waves the color of pearls.

In her office in Petit Chapeau Crea switches the eview back to the news, turns away, and lets the tears come.

That evening Tati tells Leon, "We didn't really connect." They are bent over their plates at long tables by the kitchen tent, burr of voices around them. "We talked, but it was all argument and misunderstanding. I was trying to reach for her, trying so hard."

"You need to go," says Leon. He puts down his fork to massage her neck. "I want you to go."

"No you don't," she says.

She brings loving fingers to his rough cheek, to his hair that wisps gray and white over his sunburned forehead tracked with deep lines. Ever since he showed up at her house a year ago, toting that mangled cake box and mumbling something about knowing her brother, she's felt she can breathe again. Her hunger for Crea and Fair, and her longing to have a home again, ache deeply. But she's sure that being without Leon would break her heart.

"It's been a couple of years now," he urges, "since you've seen them. You could go and come back, right? It's eating at you. I can see it."

She smiles at him, at his concern. It hasn't been easy for Leon to emerge from protective cool to allow devotion. Even now he sometimes sails away from her emotionally as if on a voyage, returning confused by her resentment. There are many things she's given up trying to explain to him.

She says, "I love you."

Music starts, sporadically at first. One guitar, then another. Hand drums, harmonicas, a flute, a violin. Someone sings along, and soon blossoms a concert of sorts, small children bouncing and swooping in dancing twirls. The sky is a serene splay of stars.

At about the same time in the grand mansion on Lake Massawippi, Crea in a strapless silk gown sitting at her vanity table turns to her husband and says, "I talked to my mother today. She wants to wait until her friend Leon can come too."

He's putting final touches to his dress uniform in front of the tall mirror in their lush hushed bedroom. Tonight they will preside over yet another elegant banquet.

"Fine," he answers abstractedly. But she knows he heard very well. What he means is, let's not talk about it. "Right now I've got to concentrate on this attack at Coburn. The Americans are after the water. If your mother is that infatuated with her man, she'll have to wait. It's her choice."

He comes to put his hands on her bare shoulders, squeezing too hard, brings his face down level with hers. The smile she gives him in the mirror is wan but he accepts it, kisses the nape of her neck.

"You look ravishing. Keep the general's doddering wife entertained please, as you know so well how to do, my dear."

"They're living in a refugee camp," she dares to persist.

"And did you order meringues to go with the brandy?"

○

Zoria is huge. One of her thighs alone is the size of a pig. Yet, though she waddles, has to bring her feet forward sideways in order to walk, her mountainous bulk seems somehow compact, sumo-stolid. There she is this Easter morning, parading with slow pomp at the head of her attendants, grand in billowing red robes, the gold upside-down cross that is her icon emblazoned across her panoramic chest. Zorian guards have cordoned off the crowd to a distance and stand stonily at intimidating intervals, but as she advances Zoria acknowledges cheers and hallelujahs with lofty smiles and solemn waves. Trumpets sounding, she ascends the stage decked with red and gold flags, takes her place on the throne.

"The good news!" blares Zoria. Her voice is a breathy rasp. "The good news is Jesus is coming. Jesus is coming!"

The crowd cheers for a whole minute. Dawn's last pastels fade into the rising sun, which bathes the guru in a halo of light. Most of the camp has gathered here, standing or sitting on the ground, bright-eyed in the cooled morning air. Families grouped proudly, children carefully dressed and combed, nobody a stranger in the exhilaration and dread of the occasion.

Tati hovers to one side. Leon would not budge from his cot, announcing that he's sick so he can't attend. It's not that anyone would try to force him, or even officially reprimand him, it's just that increasingly people think if you are Zorian you have status, clout, virtue, and if you are not, then what are you? Some kind of subversive? More and more, stepping outside the mainstream carries with it ominous suspicion, risk of harassment by the local military. True patriots toe the line. The national elections have been put off once again, and each time the excuses get flimsier, as if it's no longer worth the effort to convince anyone. Besides, now that the federal government has been streamlined with corporate officers and structures, it's clear that frequent elections interfere with economic efficiency. Zoria's gospel focuses folks on their souls, leaving the governing to those who know how.

This morning on the way back to their tent after breakfast, Tati had been annoyed with Leon, angry even.

"Don't you care if we get into trouble?" she cried. "It won't hurt you to stand there."

"Yes it will. It will hurt me to stand there and watch that woman operate. Building that damn stage was about my limit."

Knowing their tent would be full of people festooning themselves for Zoria, Tati and Leon stopped and drew aside. Night's darkness lingered in corners between tents but the dusty ground sparkled with pink sunlight.

"I specifically want to not be there," Leon pursued. "A virtue of omission, you might say," he added with a small smirk.

"Damn! Wasn't it enough to trash the guru yesterday? Don't think that won't get around. Someone will report you. It doesn't take much to get labeled a security risk. All we need is for you to end up in detention!"

"So? So?" His attempt at humor rebuffed, he got testier. Braced his legs wide apart, glowered down at her. "What happened to your precious principles all of a sudden, Tatyana?"

"Safe and sound, thank you very much. I just don't need to flaunt them in everybody's face."

But she was not feeling as pert as she sounded. She suddenly only wanted to wrap her arms around him, be at peace. Instead she tilted her head and added petulantly, "Well, I'm going. Do whatever you want."

When he turned away, she felt her blood go with him.

Trumpets, cymbals, and drums thunder a strident hymn with the refrain, "Zoria saves!"

"I ask you, my people," Zoria declaims, "I ask you. Does God love you?"

A roar of "yes" echoes in fervent response.

"Of course he does," Zoria shouts heavenward, arms lifted high so that her balloon face is cupped by the gold inverted cross on a sea of crimson. The trumpets sound again.

"My children, my precious ones, do not despair! All you need is faith. You will suffer no more, and Jesus will not suffer again, but will stay with us always. I will bring you back the Son of God, who will be born unto me. The time is coming, the time is coming!"

After another ecstatic roar from the crowd, Zoria frowns and raises a fist.

"But first, my children, you must repent. Woe unto those unbelievers who lie to you, who say it was our great industries and our great way of life that ruined the earth! Woe to the unbelievers! Jesus when he comes will shrivel them to ashes and send them straight to Hell. Straight to Hell! But you, dear little ones, you see your sins, don't you? Come, my children, weep, bow down in your sinfulness. Zoria is here! For my little ones, only shining blissful Heaven. Come! Come to Zoria, come to be saved!"

A rising tide of shouts and sobs. One by one men, women, and children file up on the stage. Into a coffin-shaped box they drop money, rings, watches, family heirlooms snatched up hastily in their flight northward. As they kneel before her, Zoria grandiosely baptizes each one, from a basin of water said to be her very own teardrops, shed for all.

Tati watching thinks, there must be two hundred of them at least, people she knows are good, caring, intelligent. Are they crazy? She turns away, as from a desecration.

She strides off seething, but stops outside the chapel. Of course it's filled with the sick — she knows the smells and sounds in there too well. On one side there's a particularly beautiful round stained glass window depicting St. Francis surrounded by colorful birds. When she had a brief bout with dysentery just after Christmas, she spent several days lying there gazing at the gentle monk. At first because of her high fever they had feared she might have the mutated ebola rumored to be devastating the south, so she was even in her acute misery intensely grateful. Now she lifts her face to the window again. I know you are here, she tells God, thank you.

The large tent is deserted except for Leon. He's sitting in their corner, where they've moved their two cots together and hung up a sort of curtain. He drops his book and stands to embrace her. They don't say a word, their passion rises fast. Tati gives her breasts to his lips, her hands caressing his groin, his back, bringing him to her. The warm pull of his nursing, their fingers stroking, pulsing. Bare body against body, open mouth on open mouth. They don't need to whisper their cries this time, but instead broadcast them boldly like music.

In the afternoon Tati watches Zoria parade out of the camp, amid more trumpets and cheering. The great guru wedges into a gold-trimmed white limousine, which is accompanied by a truckload of stern Zorians guarding the spoils. Both vehicles disappear down the road in a cloud of brown dust.

The crowd stares after them until the dust has settled. Then they turn away hanging their heads, regarding each other sadly. Tati too feels the sense of pointlessness left in Zoria's wake. What now? The drama they've all concentrated on for weeks is over. Bland deprivation and anxiety are back as their only focus. She walks slowly past the empty stage, transformed from its grandeur into the hastily nailed together mismatched planks it really is, a ramshackle symbol of loss.

Tati tries an image of shining Crea, arms around little Fair, which usually brings up her spirits. But it's a shabby picture today, frayed. Doesn't do the job. She finds shade on the stage steps, sits looking out over the tents to the hills and blank blazing sky. Soon she must show up at the kitchen to help prepare potatoes and turnips, though her hands are still chafed from last time. She takes off her hat and wipes away sweat, licks the stale salt from her lips and pulls a measured gulp from her canteen. Her next eview date with Crea isn't for another month now. They can't even write to each other, the mail system is so wildly undependable.

In answer to her yearning a vivid memory springs up, disturbing. When Crea was seven, it must have been the summer of 2015, they were all still living contentedly in Northport, Martin pleased with his new teaching job. Erosion of Long Island had not yet reached public awareness, and Tati was sure her darling little house would be their home forever. She'd pared her architectural work down to part time, reveling in motherhood. One day she was puttering in the kitchen, through the glass doors watching the children in the yard. The little plastic pool, in the shade of the old dogwood, was filling with water from the hose wielded by Denny Talbot. The Talbot boys, Denny about nine and his smaller brother, had been invited from across the street to cool off. Crea's bathing suit was pink with white polka dots, and already getting a bit too small for her.

Tati went to the table to make a note to herself to shop for a new one, turned back and froze. Denny was gleefully aiming the spurt of hose directly at Crea's crotch. She was writhing and giggling with pleasure. Denny kept this up for some time, now and then stealing a crowing conspiratorial look at his little brother. Crea danced into the spray, keeping it between her legs, shaking her blond curls, lifting her rosy face in laughter to the sky. The scene was so sensual, almost indecent. Still, Tati did not stop them. There was a beauty in it, and a privacy, that kept her out. And she told herself that the sexuality she saw was her own adult imagination.

But to her consternation, she still had the scene in her head when Martin came home that evening. She watched with new eyes as he embraced and caressed his daughter, who responded with adoring looks and eager narratives about her day. Tati had always been proud that her husband and child were so close. A swell of confusion edging on panic made her curt with both of them. It only abated that night when she donned her

flimsy negligee and seduced Martin vigorously. She still remembers her relief in feeling the hard pulse of his penis in her hand, his startled passion.

Suddenly like dawn, after all these years Tati recognizes fully how
devastating Martin's later depression must have been for their daughter.
He shut himself up away from them, from everyone who loved him. He
became a zombie. Tati in her own pain had tried to distract and protect
Crea from this unpleasantness in many motherly ways, but she hadn't en-
visioned Crea's loss as great or greater than her own.

Tati's tears come to her eyes hot and sharp with remorse.

◯

About a week later at dinner, Tati and Leon are hungrily devouring
potato stew when a man at the next table suddenly stands, staggers, and
slumps to the ground. Everyone briefly freezes in various poses of eating.
A cry from a woman who has knelt beside him, "He's burning up!" Fever!
Fear wins over concern. The man's table is deserted in a breath. He lies
alone in a great empty swath. Soon a medic appears, examines the man
with increasingly frantic gestures, shouts, "Get him out of here!"

But there is silence and nobody moves. Leon has pushed Tati behind
him. Holding onto his arm and pressed tight against him, she can feel his
tense trembling, his muscles poised for some kind of action but paralyzed
too. Faces all around are blanched and petrified, bunched up around them
and around the circle separating them from the stricken man, like a stadi-
um set up for watching. Children start to wail, picking up the sound from
each other, joining in the chorus to express what their parents feel, howls
of warning and despair.

Finally Leon goes to the table, gets their bowls of stew, brings hers to
Tati, and they both begin backing away. No heroism here. As they hurry
off they are jostled by the retreat of the panicked crowd. They turn once
to see the victim being pushed onto a stretcher. They hear the terrifying
word, "ebola."

The next night troops come to seal off the camp. People who had
already left are brought back. The quarantine will last until the disease
burns itself out. Later that morning Tati dares to approach the barbed wire
fence, hulking tanks, uniformed men with venomous looking weapons.
She's peering over them trying to see if she can glimpse the pink flurry
of apple trees. Somehow, if only she can, things may be all right. But no,
they are out of sight. The soldier directly in front of her, standing so ag-
gressively with his weapon as if poised for battle, is a boy not more than
fifteen. She smiles at him, but there is nothing in his eyes.

The hastily crafted stage is found to be the best shelter for the quickly
multiplying numbers of sick. The cots sit in rows under the planks, pro-

tected with only partial success by tarps from the feverish sun. Everyone has to take turns at ministering to the patients. Tati and Leon too, in pity and dread. Although there is no available antibiotic, they must have water, must be cleaned.

One exhausting day Tati climbs to the top of the stage, purposefully stands exactly where she remembers Zoria had posed in all her glory. From this spot, Tati can actually make out the apple trees' bright cloud. Her spirit sucks at their beauty, their reminder of lost times, as if they can give back her life.

Episode 5

Tati's Badge

Tati's feet in the red suede shoes are propped up on the dashboard, her hand on Martin's thigh as they speed past Plymouth. The radio pulses a song with a heavy drum beat, Martin booping his lips in sync, Tati keeping time on his jeans with her palm. The memory of their weekend with her mother is mercifully fading, already has lost some of its pity and pain.

"Cool shoes," Martin says, to please her.

She laughs in thanks. The shoes are a personal statement in this spring of 2003. Not brand name but with all the trappings of good running shoes, and bright rose red. With her amber blond hair and pink skin, red is not her color, at least so her mother always said. But she's even wearing a red sweater today. She curls her feet from side to side in admiration, saying, "How can she be so brainless, so helpless. She's hardly fifty, perfectly healthy..."

"Still not bad looking either. She just can't adjust to losing your father."

"He walked out eight years ago for God's sake. And it's not like she hasn't had dates. Such as they are. Freaks most of them. But still."

"She grew up in the 60s," Martin tries. "Women identified with their men in those days. She was really dependent on him."

But Tati rejects his sociological slant, boils instead into rage at her father. "The creep," she seethes. "She was a wonderful wife, did everything for him. Why, why? The bastard."

Martin takes her hand that has become a fist, massages it flat, lays it back on his leg, moves it slowly to his groin.

"Relax," he reminds her. "It's over. It was fine. We'll be home in an hour."

Dear Martin, wise Martin, sexy Martin. She squeezes him in time to the music.

He says, "Let's take the next exit."

"No way, I have too much work to do. Three projects before classes end."

But he hears instead her acquiescent sigh, and turns off the highway. Around a curve suddenly instead of roaring cars a hush, a thick splay of spring-green trees, intermittent half-hidden houses beyond wandering driveways, golden oceans of daffodils.

They park and climb a small hill to amble through a meadow where only a barn appears in the far distance. Birdsong, sweet air, sunlight pure and scintillating as water. Under a mountainous tree they spread their jackets, roll down on them giving out little laughs and cries, stirring odors of earth and new grass. Martin peels her sweater up, laps at her neck and breasts.

Her open eyes are blind at first, but gradually lime-colored branches shifting against bright sky come into focus, and then the face of a deer. Broadly antlered, muscle-shouldered, he has stopped motionless a dozen feet away, fixing them with a deep brown gaze. Holding tight to Martin, her eyes close reluctantly. But when she opens them again later as they lie quiet, the buck remains standing there. Still catching her breath, she starts to tell Martin to look but stops. The enormous peaceful eyes are reaching straight into her being, keeping her suspended. Martin is still resting inside her, so she is also him, both together caught up in the gentle yet emotionless stare.

When Martin eases away, kissing her shoulder dreamily murmuring, the buck turns and takes off in a breath, as if all his bulk and muscle were mere air. She folds Martin's damp drooping sex into her hand tenderly. Its mighty power momentarily stilled, affectionately she conceives it as a small weak animal in need of comforting.

Back in the car, she tries to explain her communication with the deer, both earthbound and otherworldly. But the words fall so short she scraps them for gasps and gestures. Martin laughs at her transports.

"You were turned on," he accuses, "I'll bet the old stag was too. Watching us humping!"

Tati cries, "You don't get it!" but she knows she can't give him the same gift. If she keeps on trying he will only be vulgar about it.

After he drops her off in Cambridge she slowly climbs the stairs to her apartment, dreading her roommate's chatter, amazed again at how empty she feels when parting from him, as if her core is gone. She's never been in love before, not like this, and its trance has thrown her off balance. Tati is strong, bold, direct. She resents the bonds of passion, her own embrace of them.

She warms up leftover Chinese takeout, shuts her bedroom door resolutely, brings up the paper she's writing that's due Wednesday. Graduate school is proving to be both easier and less fun than her college years. She re-reads the first draft, is drawn again into her theories about architecture in the 1920s. But then she makes the mistake of checking her email. A message from her father.

"Hi Tati honey — hey, your old dad will be 60 (yes six oh!) in just a few weeks, so please come and help me celebrate instead of cry. Stay with us, party, catch up with each other. We're looking forward. Love, Dad and Del."

Love Del! Doesn't he know she despises the woman? Everything from her butchy haircut to her ridiculously asexual name. Tati deletes the message hurriedly but the rage stays.

The cruelest moment of all had come when Tati and her brother and mother sat down to dinner for the first time after he'd left them. Nobody had thought to rearrange the table, and here was this empty chair, this gaping hole, that they all stared at as they tried to eat. There were supposed to be four of them, there always had been four of them, this was some kind of vicious joke. Tati's mother soon dissolved in tears, Ned banged things around the table, threw down his chair and stomped upstairs. Tati, sixteen and fed up with everything anyway, stormed out of the house and went to get laid by Johnny Foster. He was more than willing and it was fun for ten minutes, but as solace it didn't work. She wandered back home a few hours later to find her mother asleep at the table, hair streaming in congealed spaghetti sauce.

Del. It's all her fault. Some twenty years younger than her father Ray, Del is a professor of film studies who makes documentaries. Short, brash, sharp nosed, she laughs too loud and wears purple lipstick. The woman bewitched and deceived her father, Tati decided back then and believes it still. What other explanation can there be?

"Honey," said Ray at the time to a seething Tati, "try to understand. Your mother and I…"

"Just don't get along any more," Tati finished sarcastically. "I know, you told me a million times."

"Look, it's hard for me too," he started, but stopped when she yawned. "Okay, I'm sorry, I really can't explain it. You know I love you and Ned as much as ever. I'll be around, we'll get together a lot. Come on, give daddy a hug."

But Ray did not get a hug that day or any day since.

◯

"Can you believe it?" Tati challenges Martin the next afternoon. They've met for coffee in Davis Square after he taught his class at Tufts. "He expects me to visit them!"

"I can't believe you've never been to his place."

"Nope. He comes here to Boston, when he comes. Not often. Ned goes there, but not me."

People scurry in the street under a sudden rain burst, umbrellas shooting open in various colors, purple, paisley, orange, red. But the sky is still bright. It will be quick. She sips warm cappuccino, looks at Martin. He's wearing his professor outfit, a tie, crisp white shirt. They don't suit his bearish shoulders, unkempt hair, broad brooding face. He looks marvelous in flannel work shirts, or no shirt at all, hairy chested. But his long tapered poetic hands reveal his true nature, dreamy, a philosopher.

He startles her by saying, "Hey babe, I don't mean to upset you, but how about giving the guy a chance?"

"What the hell do you mean?"

"He hasn't committed a crime, for God's sake."

She stares at him coldly while her heart is beating hot with betrayal, his as well as her father's. Can it be that this man she loves does not share her soul's greatest outrage?

She says through compressed lips, "He abandoned my mother. He abandoned his wife and children."

Martin raises his eyebrows. "Gothic."

"What? Gothic? How dare you make fun of my pain? It's worse than a crime what he did, it's an insult to humanity, it's blasphemy. Listen here, mister smart ass, you have parents who stick together like glue, you have no idea what we went through, you just don't know. How can you judge me like this? Is that what you really think? That I should go all mush-headed and forgive him?"

"Calm down, Tatyana. It's been eight years and listen to yourself! Sure, he's your father. But he's a man too. Can't you try and see that?"

"A man? Is that what men do then, in your so smart opinion? Abandon their families, waltz off with any younger woman who comes along?"

"I mean, he's human. If you could see him as just that small, I think it would help. You're so damn angry! I just don't like to see you so eaten up by it."

Tati says calmly, "Go fuck yourself," gets up and stalks out into the rain.

The pavement is awash and head down she watches as her sandals soak, feet starting to feel naked wet. Hair slicks to her head, drips in her eyes. She walks fast, nowhere in particular. But, focused as she is on aimlessness, she finds herself half an hour later in front of Martin's house. His apartment is on the third floor. She stares at his name on the mailbox along with those of his roommates, and at herself reflected in the glass pane of the door. Her angular face, small nose, wide eyes, facile mouth, wearing an expression of acute misery. She sits down on the steps. The rain has stopped and the sky is white blue. Sparrows alight in a spindly tree in front of her and begin to sing intently, tiny brown and tan striped bodies straining with the effort, fluffing their still drying feathers, beaks full open to give entirely. This generosity, this oneness with their song, is to Tati more sad than soothing.

Humiliated, she realizes that even in her fury she can't run away from Martin, her love just won't let her. Her love has coerced her, wrestled her to submission. She's horrified to find she can't bear turning away from him. Because she is right, of course. He doesn't understand, has done her great wrong. But shockingly that doesn't matter. She waits, cries a little, blows her nose, combs her hair, gets up and paces for a while, sits and waits some more. Then at a sudden thought, she rings his doorbell.

In an instant, he has opened the door wide. She can't read his face. Are there tears in his eyes? As soon as she tentatively holds out her arms, his mouth is on her mouth. One of his roommates is watching television in the living room but they rush past him and shut the door to Martin's room, falling against it into each other.

○

Tati is on the train to New York. Going to see her father after all, against her heart's screaming refusal. Even as she sits here, coffee cup in hand, watching Boston recede, she can't believe she's doing this. At Back Bay more people pile on, the Friday morning train that's always busy. Asphalt gives way to sparkling water, the harbor, boats and seagulls, more and more trees. In the paper Tati reads about killing in Iraq, an oil spill off Cape Cod, another code orange terrorist alert, floods in Tennessee, and continuous wildfires in California. She gives up on the news and sets up her laptop to work on the last assignment of the semester, but soon she's staring out the window again. Vista after vista of wide water opens out as they pass through Rhode Island, rocky and sandy shores, ducks, marinas, kids fishing on a dock, houses with back yards. In Connecticut the white and mauve and nubile yellow-green of spring trees give way to darker summer leaves, wooded clutches dense. Under her the train's rhythm soothes.

Why is she going? Not only for Martin, surely. Some kind of masochistic urge to punish herself, see how much pain she can bear? This is not like her. She usually knows what she wants and sets out to get it. Now confusion, fear.

Lying in Martin's bed after their lovemaking that day when she'd walked out on him into the rain, Tati had said, "You're right, I should go visit my father. I will."

"No, babe, no." Gently he smoothed back her hair still damp with rain and sweat. The CD player was pumping the Bruce Springsteen he had put on to drown their sounds. "You're right to be angry with him. I didn't mean to deny that. Hey, I was an insensitive clod."

Tati shifted under the tangled sheet to wrap one leg across his thighs, murmured "I love you," sang with the music, "I just want to feel you in my arms, and share a little of that human touch...," went to sleep.

Later, when they woke in the lavender light of spring dusk, and she mentioned that she was having trouble finding someone to replace her roommate who was leaving, Martin said, "You know, you don't really have to go that far to find someone."

"Why?"

"Don't tell me it hasn't occurred to you. We should live together."

She propped up on an elbow, alarmed. "My God, I'd never get any work done."

"My lease here is up in June." He was grinning. "Let's do it, Tatyana."

As the train passes through Rye, anticipation of the intensity and spice of New York City begins charging the atmosphere with eclectic electricity. Soon the views turn ugly — giant parking lots and pocks of dirty oil-streaked water, along the tracks discarded tires, plastic bags, rusted fencing, barbed wire, grocery carts, shells of cars. Suddenly on the right, beyond the jowl-to-jowl roofs, looms the famous giant skyline, radiant and unnerving. Tati's pulse responds. She catches the excitement like a ball, throws it back, takes up the challenge, puts on lipstick, switches to a more sophisticated jacket. She'll spend tonight at her father's, then escape to her friend Posy's for a rollicking Saturday night.

Shouldering her backpack, she strides out along Eighth Avenue. Hazed sunlight, dust motes sparking brittle dry air. Press of people in every direction, mass of faces. After twenty blocks Tati stops in a café and orders iced coffee. She's in Greenwich Village now, with only five or so blocks to go according to her map, but she dawdles. She imagines them waiting for her, lions in the lions' den.

When she was twelve, Tati's father took her to the circus all by herself. She still remembers the acrobats and elephants, one particular pair of acrobats switching swings in mid-air, and one particular elephant in a gigantic pink hat dancing very briefly on two legs. But what she remembers much more vividly is being out alone with her father, and the considerate way he treated her, like a person. At home he was always so busy, just starting the computer business that would make them almost rich for a while, so she was nervous and thrilled to find him paying such attention to her personally. She found herself telling him about the teacher she liked and the one she hated, the friend she missed who had just moved away, her hopes for her soccer team. In her special velvet shirt and best jeans, she felt like a grownup sitting beside him, even though she had brought her plush monkey Jive along. Jive was useful because when she didn't know what to say, he could talk nonsense and save the day.

Maybe it would have been better, Tati now reflects bitterly, if her father had never tried to be her friend. The pain of her longing later would not have been so acute.

She finds the small dead end off Christopher Street easily. Trees, flower boxes, human-scale nattily decorated doorways. In front of her father's house a little fenced area with rose bushes budding red. She's suddenly self-conscious about her funky skirt and worn backpack, hair that hasn't been cut in months loose below her shoulders. In a fury at her own fears, she jabs the doorbell.

"Tatyana!"

He stands there radiantly holding out his arms. Del is nowhere in sight. Tati allows herself to be hugged.

"Hey," he crows, "you look wonderful, wow. Was the trip ok? Fast train?"

She hasn't seen him for three years, but he looks just the same, tall and loose limbed, with her own wide hazel eyes, her brother's bulbous nose. His hair is gray but still thick, with a long boyish forelock that he strokes back frequently to no avail. As he jogs ahead of her down the long hallway she catches sight of a red and white living room on the right, red sofas strewn with white toss pillows, large splashed oil paintings. Straight ahead is a kitchen and glass doors leading to a garden, but Ray leads the way upstairs to a little bedroom at the back. On the dresser squares of color in mismatched frames turn out to be photos of herself and Ned, with and without their father, in poses meant to convey family bliss.

"Here's your room, hope you like the décor. Closet here, bathroom down the hall on the left. Look at this picture, do you remember that time I took you kids sailing on Wellfleet Bay? Regular hurricane came up. But did we care?"

"It was fun, Dad," she replies, looking stupidly at the old photo, her perky preteen face. "I remember, sure."

His strenuous efforts to be welcoming make her feel very tired. She tells him to her own surprise that she wants to change, take a shower. Of all the times she has conceived this moment, she never thought she'd chicken out. She had hoped she would dare to confront him, tell him bitter truths, get him to confess, apologize. Cut cruelly through his façade, make him bleed.

Clean and freshly dressed, she stands combing her hair looking out at the long narrow garden, lilac fists in lusty bloom, quavering birch tree at the end, round wrought iron table with chairs. In one of the neighboring gardens two yellow cats are chasing each other. Tati decides she'll have to make herself at home with the nauseous lump in her throat, because it won't go away.

She's helping her father chop vegetables in the kitchen when Del breathlessly arrives. Nothing Del does is quiet, the place immediately fills with her presence. She plops an overflowing briefcase on the floor, embraces Tati, who keeps her arms at her sides, and kisses Ray on the mouth.

"You are so good, baby," she croons at him, "to be doing the salad, it's the hardest part. He makes a spectacular salad. And avocado? Fantastic."

The doors are open to the garden sucking in sweet hot earth smells, the heady pulse of lilacs. Del's forehead is shiny with sweat. Her dark hair is cut close up from her neck like a man's, though curly wings over her ears are allowed to assert femininity. She's wearing a thin gold choker and earrings with crimson centers, a bejeweled watchband. Her shirt is white and plain, but opened down the front far enough to hint at plump pink breasts. She has small blunt hands with short fingers, big hips unapologetic in close-fitting trousers. Her mouth is large with large teeth, her smile continuous and wet. Behind her glasses large black eyes move quickly looking, or thinking fast.

They eat outside at the garden table draped with a lacy tablecloth.

"Your father tells me," Del grins at Tati, "that you enjoy swimming." Her voice though loud is soft, symphonic.

"Well, I don't have much time for it these days. But I get to the pool when I can, and of course in the summer we go to the beach quite a lot."

"With your boyfriend?"

"Martin, yes."

"He teaches at Tufts, I understand. He and I will have to compare notes on student misbehavior." She laughs heartily, holds up her wine glass for Ray to refill, and when he does they gaze at each other as if neither has ever seen such a marvelous creature.

Tati swallows with difficulty. Del rests her hand on Ray's shoulder while her swift eyes hold Tati's dazed.

Ray starts to talk about the time he taught Tati to swim at age four. Tati has no memory of this, in fact she thinks she learned at the Y. It's a wonderful story, though, and she tries to believe it's true.

"So she was kicking like this," he chortles, "and suddenly lets go. She's flailing, but she's on her own! I was proud of her, I tell you. Your mother was proud, too. She said you were a regular little athlete. And you know, she was right. Look at the gymnastics medal you got."

Mention of her mother in this casual almost intimate way alarms Tati, churns further confusion. Unprepared, she's still frantically searching for a way to fit this element into the picture, when Del starts talking about her health club.

"I do the machines, the bicycle and the treadmill," she confides, chewing tomato vigorously. "Keeps me decently trim."

Ray laughs to her suggestively. "Indecently too!" Prompting Del's hand to weasel pale and stout into his large palm. Their two hands lie together on the tablecloth gently writhing intertwined.

Tati gazes intensely at the lilacs, gulps something about dogwood and magnolias in Cambridge.

"Sure must be beautiful there now," Ray agrees heartily, beaming at Tati as if he were not searing her heart. "Got a nice apartment too, right?"

"Martin and I are going to live together," she hears herself announcing, to her delight. Her words empower her even before Del and Ray start and stare, hands springing apart.

He intones doubtfully, "That sounds serious."

"Wedding bells?" queries Del.

"No, nothing like that," Tati takes great pleasure in assuring them, "we just want to live together, for awhile, for fun."

They both look at her more closely. Del is the first to regain her equilibrium, quip, "Why not?" with a juicy grin.

"I'd like to meet him," Ray suggests.

Melted by his solicitous possessiveness, however fleeting, Tati replies affectionately, "He wants to meet you too."

After having thus righted the power imbalance at least outwardly, Tati is able to tolerate the rest of the evening. There is even a moment that she enjoys, when she and her father go back out into the garden leaving Del in the kitchen. The moon is up and they can make out some constellations, which he explains quietly to her as if he never had before, a dozen times in the old days.

"The big dipper, there with the handle…Orion the hunter with his diamond belt and sword…Venus, star of stars…"

Staying with his voice, looking not at him but only up at the sparkled darkness, this could be years ago again, she still that unsuspecting little girl.

But when she climbs into bed reeling with exhaustion, Tati is consumed above all, above all the tempest and confusion, with a roiling sense of loss. Her rage has been wrested from her; she bleeds where it was. She's no longer her own heroine. She carries no banner, no special stigmata. Her life will happen in the usual way — Martin, marriage, children, work, age — all of that, death too. Acceptance pierces like grief.

She expects her father to notice, the next day at breakfast, that she is different. But of course he doesn't. He's as affectionate, casual, and cheery as before, as if he spent a perfectly serene night, as if he never heard of sorrow, as if he never faced himself in the middle of the night or saw his own unrecognized face in the mirror.

Episode 6

Knots

"That's why we have to shoot so many," explains Marguerite. "Because deporting them takes too much fuel."

The kitchen is a flurry of activity an hour before dinner, and Marguerite has just tasted the sole with the delicate dab of a fork. She barks instructions in French at the cooking crew, continues without pause in English, "but they usually save the children."

Tati stands awkwardly in the doorway, trying to nod noncommittally, not succeeding. She knows that instead her eyes are aghast at the housekeeper's casual pronouncements.

Crea hurriedly chimes, "Oh look at the time, mom, we've got to go get gussied up! Come on."

As Crea steers away a stunned Tati, Marguerite cheerily calls after them, "There won't be a lot of them left soon anyway, thank the good Lord. We're rounding them up pretty quick."

"Crea," Tati begins as they climb the broad stairs. "What she said. They shoot the refugees?"

"Well sometimes, when they catch them. But lots of them get away, mom, don't worry. Now what shall you wear tonight? Don't you love the black and silver gown we got for you yesterday?"

In Tati's room the drapes have been pulled and the bed turned down. All is pastel blue and lace, shaded lights, cushioned fabrics.

"Crea, it's Americans she's talking about. I mean, isn't it?"

"Well, it's people who have crossed the border into Canada illegally, since it was closed in 2043. I don't know what else to say. I know it's terribly sad, but be reasonable. We can't let them all in, too many are here already."

"Them? I'm one of them. So were you!"

The two women are facing each other on either side of a long mirror. Gray-haired Tati angular and gaunt, Crea spun gold, supple. Crea takes a breath to protest, but shrugs instead.

"Hey, mom. I know. I'm sorry."

Sorry! Tati has only been in her daughter's house for three days, and already they are confronting each other. Tati has vowed a million times to take it easy, to let whatever comes come, to be a fountain of love only. Furious with herself, she steps quickly to embrace Crea, murmur, "No, I'm sorry, sweetheart." Feeling her child's soft warmth that she dreamed of so often in the drab refugee tent in Vermont where she lay all those infinite nights.

As Tati undresses, she adds with apologetic chuckles, "I'm so naïve. I guess I was just surprised that your housekeeper has such violent views. But lots of people do now, don't they? And she's being loyal to her homeland, I'll say that for her."

"She's loyal to us, too, she thinks Han is God's gift. And she's so patient with Fair."

Crea shakes out the shimmering dress and helps Tati slip it over her head. Tati stares in the mirror in amazement.
"Like Cinderella," Tati laughs. Watches herself laugh, an honest to goodness, hearty, look-at-gorgeous-me laugh, like the old days.

Now twelve year-old Fair is in the doorway, breathless as usual.

"It was too muddy to take the horses to the woods, but we circled the pasture. Can I call Naomi now? I practiced already."

Tati watches her child and grandchild negotiating, alternately glancing at her own elegant imposture in the mirror. Fair is small but lanky, with tiny budding breasts lumped like afterthoughts under her shirt, red-brown braids awry. She has her dead father's Irish leprechaun bow mouth always on the edge of a smile or a song, or a sneer. A mouth of messages even when silent. Crea is no match for her.

"But mom I went over the Mozart twice, really. Naomi's mother needs to know if I'm going to the game with them."

"It's raining again, sweetheart. They can't play soccer in the mud, can they?"

When Crea was that age, she was already too beautiful. Boys climbed trees outside her bedroom window just to hope for a glance. Tati would have to chase them off herself, Martin already too deep into depression to care. Martin, who when she met him was so poetic a philosopher that she first fell in love with his passion for ideas. Sex with him was astounding then, he seemed a foreordained soul mate. She remembers her stunned ecstasy, their wild limbs, insatiable. Tati in those days, dedicated architecture student, was equally consumed with love, lust, and the joy of landscape modeling. Crea was born out of love, certainly. The saddest thing for Tati was that she stopped respecting Martin long before she stopped loving him.

Crea and Fair have raised their voices and Tati steps judiciously to the window to watch the streaming February rain. The grounds are brightly lit, so water-blurred light reveals rivers of mud beveling the ground, the high fence looming beyond. It was raining with hurricane craziness when she arrived, in a limousine that picked her up from the border outpost. When she first saw it, the fancy car seemed so incongruous that she kept on standing there hugging her little bag of belongings, still wearing the old coat that no longer buttoned across her middle, not moving even when the uniformed driver opened the door for her. The small clutch of Americans she had traveled with inched away from her as if she were royalty, alien. Even though most of them were clearly far more affluent, indeed that's the only way they could have got into Canada. But all the while feeling privileged and grateful, she felt she was entering into a delusion that she could not share.

"Oh well ok, sweetheart," sighs Crea. "You're probably right that your teacher doesn't expect perfection with the concerto yet. Go ahead and call Naomi. Just brush your hair for dinner, please."

Fair's little face is smug as pie, but Crea doesn't seem to notice. Fair tosses her head at her grandmother with a tweaked smile, and whizzes off.

"Don't know what to do with her," says Crea with tired pride.

"She's superb," Tati assures her.

"You do look a dream in that dress, mom!"

At dinner there are six guests, the men in the same blue-gray Guard uniform as Captain Hanley. He sits benign but hawk-eyed at the head of the table, possessively watching his beautiful wife Crea, resplendent in pale gold silk. The talk is briefly of the drinking water shortage and the growing power of the "barons," but quickly shifts to casual comments on the rain, offspring, social events, and wonderful food. The wine glasses are often replenished, and Tati herself begins to feel that life could just possibly be good again.

Before she falls asleep, one leg drawn up Tati rests her hand between her legs and thinks about Leon. He's lying on his cot in their tent in the Burlington refugee camp, thinking of her, she knows. Maybe he's reaching over to touch her empty cot, maybe his hand is on his groin, too. Missing him stings her. But she's now feeling more confident that Han will manage to get passage for him before summer, the summer heat that starts in Vermont already in April and is so devastating to bear in those tents. Captain Hanley, rumored to be promoted to general soon, is a man of seemingly limitless power. She must ask him about it tomorrow, just for her own peace of mind. She finds sleep in embracing Leon's image, his grim old face pocked with wrinkles coming to her for kisses.

"I assure you, Tatyana," says Han the next morning, "we'll have those papers for your friend Leon in a week or so, tops."

They are standing by the glass doors in the library, looking out over the deck to the winter garden where sunlight creeps through fog. Tati is still holding her coffee cup. His hands are behind his back, legs apart. She looks up at him, his fine head with close cropped white hair, strong mobile mouth, broad shoulders with medals adorning immaculate uniform. A handsome and charismatic man. Now she understands Crea's choice better. Much as Crea's first husband David had been a charmer, he could not claim this animal magnetism.

Marguerite comes with a coffee pot, asks, "Would Madame like some more?"

Tati holds out her cup, realizing that she already takes this kind of service for granted. Marguerite, probably forty, sturdy with strong beefy hands, wears a black frilled uniform topped with a white apron. She's often noisy and nosy, but always deferential. There is nothing humble about her; she carries her servitude like a badge.

Han's eyes looking over Tati's head light up in satisfaction, so she knows before turning that Crea has entered the room. She's soft in rose cashmere, lush pale hair caught up from her neck in a twist.

She kisses her husband, announces, "We'll need to go into town soon. The weather report says it's turning very cold, all that water's going to freeze."

"Should in February," Tati notes dryly, even though she knows that any remark referring to the climate calamities that have turned the whole world upside down is socially uncouth. Denial is no longer an option, it's just that it seems rude and disloyal somehow.

Crea hugs her to show she's forgiven for this little lapse in good manners. "Want to come? It'll be nice for you to get out, see the town and countryside a bit."

Tati agrees. "But first let's have a look at your garden while the rain's stopped."

The two women go out the glass doors to the deck. It's very warm, though the sunlight has no color. Crocuses poke yellow and lavender through the mud, buds on lilac bushes are fattening green.

"It's going to get too cold for them," laments Tati.

"I hate to lose them again this year. Last spring even the willow blossoms froze."

Within the fenced grounds all the flowerbeds sport green shoots, and several trees, including an old oak large enough to support an enormous crow's nest, are starting lacy blossoms. To the right beyond the fence further up the hill, wet brown branches of more trees are netted against the watery sky. Without comment, Marguerite brings them chairs that she whisks into place with muscular grace. But Tati and Crea turn away and lean over the railing together, mourning the reckless flowers' imminent death.

"I wonder if there are any crocuses left in Concord," muses Tati. "How I miss that house."

"Me too. We had some wonderful times there, before."

"I wonder if it's standing just the way Leon and I left it. Almost two years ago now — it seems forever. Or if it's vandalized, or maybe travelers are using it. I hope somebody's there, though, so long as they don't wreck it. Not that it matters, I guess."

"Thank God you're here now, mom, safe."

Tati skirts the conventional reply, longs to say something to continue fanning the glow of their old intimate bond.

"Your husband seems a fine man," she tries.

Crea starts, takes a quick look back toward the library. Then she smiles and trills, "He is! Fair and I are so blessed. He saved us, you know. Next month will be our wedding anniversary."

Stymied, Tati doesn't answer these platitudes. Instead she goes over and closes the glass doors. She comes back, stands tall, folds her arms, and looks hard at her daughter. Crea recoils a few steps and leaves a silence, but doesn't avert her eyes.

"I miss David," she finally confesses.

Tati drops her arms and rests against the railing, waits. Crea walks back and forth a few times, head low.

"It was so sudden," Crea continues. "And on the road, where we didn't know anybody. One day there he is and then the next…a nightmare. Fair has everything here. Can you imagine what our life would have been after David died if Han hadn't rescued us? We probably would've gotten cholera too, or we'd be starving somewhere or….I'm deeply grateful to Han. He's our rock. Our hero. But, but….he's very possessive, he loves me so much, you know, he can't bear not to know where I am every minute. He's…difficult, sometimes."

"It's all been so hard for you." Neutral words, loving tone.

Crea shakes away the start of tears, tends her hair with swift fingers, says briskly, "Fair is happy. That's what counts. For me that's what counts."

O

In the limousine Tati sits facing forward, opposite Crea and Fair.

As they come through the gate saluted by Guards and continue down the drive, Fair points out a friend's house, just visible behind its own high fence.

"And that's Lake Massawippi," she adds, enjoying teaching an adult. "The shacks are all flooded out, so the people had to move."

"Where did they go?"

"Oh, they always go north of course. Everybody goes north."

"Well," Crea corrects gently, "many of them just put up new shacks on higher ground."

"My teacher says," Fair finishes with a flourish, "it's so hot in the south of the U.S., people die from just walking."

Crossing the bridge over the river that feeds the lake and climbing the next hill, they come in sight of rows of ramshackle huts, constructed out of every kind of material imaginable from planks to old tires. People stop and stare as they pass. People in shabby clothes, children without shoes. Tati had arrived in Petit Chapeau in darkness, so this is a shock.

"It's just as bad as Vermont," she murmurs. "I had no idea."

"Well, they have enough to eat," Crea says. "But heating fuel is going to be a problem when we get this cold snap."

Cold snap. The merry jargon that passes for communication, when everyone knows a fifty degree drop in temperature plus a blizzard is on the way. Tati looks her annoyance, and Crea adds, "Of course it's sad, but what can we do? We have to watch our fuel too."

"What do they do for water, drinking water?"

"Oh," pipes Fair, "it's rationed, of course. So everybody gets their share."

Crea hastens to add, "Our water's rationed too."

"But we have special water delivered," the child boasts.

After they drop Fair off at her piano teacher's house, they continue out into the countryside. Here dispersed along the road are a few houses that look like the old days, well-kept, one even with a car in the driveway. Children romping in rubber boots, parents sweeping a porch, mending a bike, a roof. To Tati it's a joy barbed with pain. Her lost world.

"It's like it used to be," she cries, straining to keep each one in sight as it passes by. "Before."

"I knew you'd like it," Crea glows.

She's so pleased with her mother's pleasure that Tati realizes guiltily how judgmental she's been. Boy, am I good at indignation, she reprimands herself harshly. And vows from now on to be more grateful and accepting.

Tati is used to the extreme weather and violent storms of recent decades, but she's still startled by the swiftness of the change that afternoon. First comes rain again, but within hours it turns to sleet and then driving snow. The wind picks up as well, so by three o'clock the snow is being driven almost horizontally across the sky. Howling whipping sounds and claps of thunder orchestrate doomsday through the elegant rooms. Even the resounding Handel harp concerto that Crea turns up loud can't dispel the ominous mood.

Passing a door in the hallway Tati hears a peculiar sound. A kind of small moaning. A cat perhaps? But they don't have a cat, do they? When she presses the door where the distress seems to be, it opens. This is Han's study, she remembers now, centered by an array of computers and video recorders, to one side a pair of comfortable chairs, and on the floor nearby Han kneeling over something. One step inside and Tati sees Marguerite on hands and knees, buttocks rising to meet Han's thrusting. Both are still in uniform, though he's in shirtsleeves, and the only flesh evident is the looming white mass of Marguerite's behind, rhythmical. Tati for a second glances away, tries to shake the sight by taking in windows, desk, machines. Meets Han's eyes, glazed with his effort, with his pleasure, looking at her. Then he catches his breath sharply and lifts his head in a throaty roar.

Tati is back in her room not knowing how she got there. It's dusk, no lights yet, only now and then a flash of lightning across the plush rug. She cowers on the edge of the bed, fists at her eyes. She tries not to know what she has seen, almost succeeds for an instant when the vile weight mercifully lifts, but plummets upon her again and she succumbs. What this means for Crea does not bring surprise. The man is what he has seemed all along. But because she had so wanted to, Tati had bought in, into the Han as hero scenario, the assured safety and well-being of Crea and Fair, his dignity and devotion. Pig, pig, she mutters.

Tati used to nurse Crea sitting in an old wicker rocking chair by the window of their cramped apartment off Prescott Street in Cambridge. The baby's skinny fingers more like claws working the flesh of her breast, the tiny avid mouth. The sweet pull at her nipple, through her deepest body. Sometimes when Tati had to go out and leave a bottle for Martin or the babysitter, her breasts would get so full they'd ache and start to leak. She would hurry into the apartment crying, only half humorously, "Where's that baby! Got to get rid of this milk!" It was still cool in October in those days, and the trees were brilliant in their colors. To Tati gazing out with her suckling baby, the flamboyant trees and bright clouds, the squirrels and birds, were more a part of their world than the people busily passing in the street.

Now Tati crosses her arms pressed against her belly, as if Crea were back in there where no hurt could reach her. No, she will not tell Crea what she has discovered. She debates the idea only long enough to picture the straits Han could reduce them all to if he chose. Besides, Tati reasons, Crea does not want to know. She would only hate the messenger. It seems to her mother, crouching here over her stomach in the dusk, that Crea's survival and even sense of identity are woven into the convoluted arrangement she has conceded.

After dinner the family gathers in the library for brandy and chocolate. Fair is trilling a cheerful piece on the piano. She's wearing a pretty dress, hair loosed from braids held curling back from her face with heart shaped barrettes. Drapes conceal the tempest raging outside the windows. Tati watches Han watching Crea. Because there were no guests tonight, he's dressed casually in a black turtleneck sweater over corduroys. He's idly turning pages of a newspaper, Crea leaning lightly on the piano. His eyes on his wife are smug, calculating, like a cat that has sufficiently wounded a bird so it can no longer escape. The cat can relax and play at capture — the real struggle is over, the prey now even perhaps a bit less appetizing.

Later on Tati is not surprised to find herself alone with Han. Crea and Fair have gone upstairs, but he remains. She peruses the bookcase, glances over to see him still sitting there. He's not pretending to read the newspaper now.

"Oh, Han, I didn't see you."

He doesn't answer. They both know very well she knew he was there. They both have been waiting for this moment.

"Well, Tatyana," he starts genially, folding his hands in an arch, "how are you enjoying your visit?"

She decides not to sit down, stands behind a high backed chair, hands steadying on the silky fabric. The word visit has not been lost on her.

"Thank you," she replies a bit woodenly. "It's wonderful to be here with Crea and Fair." She pauses to cool her anger. Getting upset will only give him the upper hand. "Don't worry, I'm not going to tell her."

Something like admiration comes into Han's hard stare. He gets up to pace, working his way closer to where she stands not moving, except to tilt her chin a little higher.

"I'm glad to hear it, Tatyana," he remarks paternally. "We all need to keep our heads these days."

"But you should be aware," she goes on defiantly, "that I think what you're doing is despicable. I don't care how much power you have over the rest of the world, my daughter's heart and her trust are not to be scorned, the love and trust of a beautiful, wonderful woman who…"

"Shut up."

He stands next to her, too close. She can sense the heat and muscle of him.

He speaks softly, leaning his face down into hers. "I'm not going to apologize, if that's what you're after, Tatyana. I'm not going to promise any changes. I do what I want, what I need. I have needs that are not anyone's affair, especially yours."

"Well then, Han, I'm not going to forget about it, if that's what you're after."

He reddens with annoyance and steps back.

"You should know," he says slowly to give his words the full weight of blows, "I won't be able to get those papers for your friend after all."

"Ah," she breathes, "so that's it."

Han is very pleased with the effect of his punishment. Tati's mouth slacks, she stumbles around the chair to sit down. Her lips are dry, she feels dizzy. He begins to pace again, hands behind his back military style, back and forth in front of her, smiling.

"I wonder," she finally says, in a voice so calm it startles him, "would you mind pouring me a bit of brandy?"

He stops to look at her. He can't believe she's not in tears. "Of course," he begrudges.

She sips the drink, gratefully feeling its burn, licks her lips and then drains the glass. She closes her eyes to focus on the calming. When she opens them, Han is sitting in his chair again across from her.

"Try to understand," he astonishes her by saying, "I have a brutal amount of responsibility. Just imagine having the lives of millions of soldiers in your hands, plus the lives of all the people under our protection. A central government chasing its tail, deadly unpredictable weather crises over and over, a 3,000 mile border threatened in a hundred strategic places every day…"

Tati leans her head against the back of the chair and appalls herself by seeing him for the first time as a human being. Cruel, calculating, arrogant, human. She starts to reply that there are no excuses, that it's his own fault if he's stressed or corrupted by his role, that people who love you are the highest responsibility, but she doesn't say a word. She comprehends that in a horrible, heart-rending way, he is right.

During the night Tati tortures herself over a decision that finally, when she realizes it with dawn, was never really in question. She will return to Burlington, to the misery and anxiety of the refugee camp, to Leon.

Marguerite strides in with morning coffee, opens the drapes, croons, "Good morning, Madame." She's as proud and ingratiating as always — of course Han has not told her they were seen. That will remain forever the secret between him and Tati, the conspiracy in some way tainting Tati too.

Episode 7

Ghost of a Chance

Mr. Simms peers out the window at Fair Franklin. She's stepping from the back of the limousine, leaning down to speak to the driver, above her knee socks the pleated skirt of her school uniform hiking toward round thighs. Mr. Simms flushes and adjusts his trousers. Up the walk she sweeps, all breasts and hips, heading for him. Of course the car will wait until she's safely inside and will return in less than an hour to whisk her away again.

A feathery man with wisps of hair and birdish bones, Mr. Simms skitters to the piano where he's deeply ensconced in trilling out Mozart when Fair enters. She shrugs off her jacket, bounds over like the child she was only yesterday, to join him on the piano bench. She smells warm.

Soon he leaves her dutifully repeating a concerto, and scampers to the back of the house. Sure enough, the men are waiting, have slipped through the unlocked door. They're wearing dark leathery coats and caps and they don't say anything. The insides of Mr. Simms turn to ice. He knows they have to bind him, too. Hit him. It has to look real. For a wild moment he thinks he'll call it off. But they're already pushing him back down the hall to the conservatory.

Two blocks away, the van is waiting. It's painted pink with a cheery sign announcing "La Patisserie Danielle" along with pictures of smiling bread. In the front sit a man and woman joking and chortling. They ignore the noises from the back, the screams and sobs, the usual.

In the conservatory, there's blood on the Mozart score. It has fallen beside a writhing Mr. Simms. Fair thrashes in the mens' grip as they gag and wrap her in a rug. They hoist her to their shoulders like a mummy.

At the same moment they trundle the girl into the pink van, her mother Crea reaches for a grape from a white bowl by the window of the library in her lovely home looking down on Lake Massawippi. Crea, beautiful wife of General Hector Hanley, a legend in his own time. To him, it is said, is owed the relative calm of this part of the southeastern border, while elsewhere skirmishes and abductions are daily fare. As a young man in the early 2020s, Han already showed the foresight and acumen he's famous for by joining the other Americans immigrating to Canada, and his star has been rising ever since.

Savoring the grape, Crea passes through to the kitchen to talk to Marguerite about dinner. She wants to make sure there will be apple tart for dessert, Fair's favorite.

Inside the back of the van it's dark and smells of vomit. Fair lands on a pile of blankets or clothes or both. The van jolts into racing motion. She feels hands working at her bindings, freeing her bit by bit. A girl with crazed eyes leans into her face and says, "Are you hurt?"

In the kitchen, Marguerite the housekeeper is stirring seafood stew and chastising the cook for adding too much dill. Crea tastes it as requested and nods noncommittally, doesn't join the fray. Her mind is on the guest list for the dinner party she and her husband are hosting this evening, Friday, March 8th, the day she'll be told that her daughter won't be home for years, if ever. Of course she will know this means the bandits have her, and she will know what that means, too.

As Fair left for school that morning Crea said to her, "Sweetpea, don't forget your lesson with Mr. Simms. And I hope you'll wear your wintergreen tonight."

Fair, every day more lovely with her burnt-red curls and coltish grace, gave an impatient groan.

"If I have to be there," she sulked, "at least let me wear my new black velvet top. At least let me look half decent."

Crea laughed and gave her daughter a swift squeeze. "You know that velvet blouse is too revealing. Han doesn't like it."

"Han doesn't think I'm a day older than when he first met me. Why do you let him run my life? He doesn't even know who I am."

"He cares for you very much," Crea responded automatically.

As the hour for Fair's return passes, and her mother begins the vague terror she fights every time her child is late, this exchange runs through her mind again and again. It's true, she thinks, Han dominates me but why Fair as well? She needles her brain probing for solutions, guiltily, with rising urgency as the minutes crawl by. But not one scenario includes confronting her husband directly.

In front of the mirror Crea dresses her soft pale hair, hearing without listening to the news about the drought that still grips the eastern seaboard from Atlanta to St. John's. Although the border has been closed to the Americans for four years now, this particularly long drought is making them desperate to the point of suicidal risks, like creeping through minefields at night.

"Shall I bring the general's cocktail in now?" asks Marguerite, closing the heavy drapes to the darkening sky.

Inside the pink van, sitting up painfully and trying to stop crying, Fair haltingly thanks her fellow captive. In a corner another girl sobs hysterically, clutched in a fetal position. They are all fifteen and bound for Baron Lemoyne's compound just south of Chicoutimi.

Lemoyne is one of the more powerful barons who have sprung up in the chaos of recent decades. So many Guards are needed to police the 3,000 mile border, it has become tacitly accepted for the barons to keep order internally. At a price. Paying lip service to patriotism and the public good, they twist the laws to suit their own interests. The numbers of their goons are increased every day by refugees who have slipped in from the

American states, especially the roving bands of teenagers called Hornets who make excellent — daring and amoral — underlings. Within a few years the barons have gone from citizen militia to mini-governments in their own right. Now they are sparring among themselves for dominance, and lately there have been armed skirmishes.

Towards midnight on a dark wooded road crusted with ice, the pink van transfers its human cargo to a horse-drawn covered wagon that resembles the countless family vehicles heading north. The van drivers pocket wads of cash and speed away.

Crea slumped in a chair screams in her half-sleep.

The following week on a brilliantly sunny morning, with Baron Lemoyne's renovated ski lodge buildings spread out splendidly in a new dusting of snow, Madame Jacqueline wakes the girls with her usual gritty cheer.

"Rise and shine my little darlings!" she calls.

If they don't tumble out of bed immediately, she prods them with her "wand," a thick pole resembling a broomstick which she claims is her cane but is never seen using as such. The wand tends to land between their legs. Mme. J. is blousy and busty and almost always dressed in red.

Fair heads for the bathroom but stops when Mme. J. keeps on poking at Maeve, who is crunched up under the covers and sobbing as usual. How can she have any tears left?

"Mme. Jacqueline, please stop," Fair ventures. "She'll get up."

Instead, Mme. J. throws back the covers, grabs at Maeve's nightgown, pushes up her legs, and thrusts the wand a few inches into her. Maeve gives a guttural cry of pain.

"If the Baron didn't want you," spits Madame, "I'd have my way with you, you mewling puking pitiful excuse for a female."

Fair strides over and grabs for the wand, which whips around and smacks her across the back. Fair hits the ground. Now Mme. J. cools; clearly she must not damage the goods. She helps Fair up, lifting her nightgown to check for bruises, stands back.

"Come on, loveys," she croons breathlessly, smugly as at a job well done. "Lots to learn today."

Fair stumbles into the bathroom, where Clementine is calmly brushing her teeth. She's the last of their predecessors, having turned eighteen and no longer of interest to the Baron. She's been sold back to her parents, so will be returning home soon. Manette, the girl who freed Fair from her bonds in the van, pulls Maeve up and practically drags her into the bathroom. But Mme. J. allows them no privacy. She even watches them while they sit on the toilet.

In the classroom, the three new girls receive their second day of instruction. Yesterday they were introduced to the "biology of the penis," so that they thoroughly understand how it is stimulated. Today they are issued plastic dildos. They sit almost primly in a semi-circle in soft chairs like movie theater seats.

"Hold it like this," Mme. J. demonstrates, "and lick the tip like this. Just like a lollipop."

They all obey.

"Now enter it into your throat, open up your throat to let it slide in."

The girls put the dildos tentatively into their mouths.

"All the way in, now. That's very good, Manette. Now constrict your throat around it. Pull it in and out. Just pretend it's candy. Yes, good."

Maeve and Fair are choking, and Maeve vomits again.

This time Mme. J. smiles. "Maeve deary," she chuckles. "It's always the soppy little wimps like you that end up the most willing."

After class, Fair manages to get Clementine alone by following her back to the dorm room. On the third floor of the lodge, the room has a spectacular view of the narrow river and forested hills beyond the guard towers and barbed-wire fence. Although the green of the forest is splotched with swaths of browning trees, and the barren river banks reveal where much more water once ran, the sight in the bright sun is serene, the sky cloudless azure.

"You'll have classes for a couple more days," Clementine replies to Fair's question. They are sitting on Fair's bed near the window. "And then you'll start serving the baron. Have you met him yet?"

"We saw him. He's fat. He's hideous."

"Well," shrugged Clementine. "That you'll get used to. Whatever they tell you to do, just do it and think about something else."

"No."

"What do you mean, no. You don't have a choice, if you ever want to see your family again."

"No, I'm not going to do it. It's humiliating. I've got to get out of here."

Clementine starts laughing, quietly but hysterically. "Nobody gets out of here. Don't you know you're a prisoner? You're a slave."

Fair stares at her. Clementine is a pretty, brittle, frozen sort of person, and her laughter abruptly stops like a machine. She clutches Fair's shoulders and hisses into her face, "Get out, oh God, get out while you can! They'll make a monster out of you!"

When Clementine has fled from her own cracked mask, Fair stays on the bed gazing at the distant hills. She pictures the bone-deep suffering of her mother, the outraged rallying of troops by her stepfather — he'll be wild with this affront to his power more than the loss of his wife's daughter — and she fears, from all she's heard, that Guards will not be truly committed to an operation that would alienate all the barons. Much will be made of this most recent abduction of young girls, but it will be all fuss and words. But her mother, what will she do? Will she find the courage to escape her own sort of bondage and conduct a real search? Perhaps. Perhaps she'll stand up to her husband and persuade him to help her. But Fair's terror keeps its grip on her gut. She finds she can't picture her mother exerting that kind of courage. Her sweet, soft mother who has grown meek under Han's reign. Small hope there.

Fair perches on the bed, growing resolve glinting her brown eyes amber. She's her father's daughter, stubborn and good at anger. She thinks of him now, summons him. When he died, Fair closed her heart safe around him. Yes, he is telling her to fight.

She chooses six o'clock. That afternoon the three girls are issued outfits, lacy revealing panties and gowns, skin-tight suits. Fair goes through the ritual aloof, as if she's up above looking down on trivia, helping Maeve cope as best she can. Manette is doing fine, she has clearly chosen the path of least resistance. When they are ordered to dress provocatively for dinner, Fair climbs into bed, pulls the covers up to her chin, and closes her eyes. Clementine is giving them tips in her offhand jaded way while Mme. J. pulls and pushes the bits of clothing to best advantage.

"What, what!" shouts Mme. J. when she sees Fair lying there.

"I'm sick," says Fair.

She feels Madame's oily breath.

"Get up. You are not sick. Get up."

And she starts in with the wand. Jabs at Fair's thighs, buttocks. But the dinner bell is ringing, and anyway she can't be completely sure, so after awhile she desists and turns her attention back to decking out her other disciples.

All night Fair tosses in pangs of hunger. They had brought a tray of food so she drinks the liquids, juice and tea, but no solids, not even soup. She lies and listens enviously to the others' slumber, ravenous. But she feels strong, pretty sure her plan will work. When she's dangerously close to harming herself, the baron will back down. She knows she's valuable: Han can easily afford to ransom her.

"It's no use," Clementine comments airily in the morning. "They can't afford to let you break the rules."

Mind weakly wandering, Fair watches the sky, long puffy scudding clouds like laughter. She imagines she's riding them, off into the sun, home. Her mother runs to the door as she rides up and leaps off, they embrace in wild joy. Wait, her father is there too! All three of them, together again.

By afternoon when Mme. J. brings the doctor, Fair's pangs have dulled to a constant ache. The doctor, an elderly woman with impressive warts, declares coldly, "She's faking it. Throw her in the isolation room. She'll come round."

During that night, Crea pacing her hushed house in sleepless suffering fitfully revisits the paths of her own life, and tells over every detail of Fair's. Growing up, Crea had wanted to be a schoolteacher, but her world had forced quite different plans. As she shuffles back and forth through the chilly rooms lit only by the intermittent flash of searchlights trained on the grounds, the belt of her robe trailing behind, the scenes rise disjointed through her exhaustion. David's face as he held infant Fair, his smug joy. The three of them dancing in a circle in the living room to Irish medleys. Fair's heart-rending wails when her music box broke. Her amazing stoicism in having to give up all her friends and everything she knew when they fled to Canada. Those terrible days when David died. Following Han into the luxurious quarters he had arranged for them. While she knew what she would have to do for this lifestyle — Han had made no secret of it — she accepted her fate with only brief hesitation. In that moment when they walked through the door onto that unbelievably soft carpet, Fair heading straight for the piano, Han turning Crea to him with a heavy hand at her waist, she felt Fair's innocent enthusiasm in contrast to her own uneasy compliance like a chasm between herself and her child.

The windows of the front parlor look out over the lake. Light is becoming a suggestion at the horizon's edge, though everything is still without color. The lake looks so cold. Not icy but steel gray, hard, lifeless. Now Crea has lost everything she loved. Even her mother is unreachable, on the other side of the invincible border. Marcel too, for his safety depends on her sacrifice of his friendship. There's a vase of silk flowers here on this table by the window, white and pink tulips and peonies. She strokes their petals, soft and chill, without scent. When Fair was thirteen they decided to cut her hair. She had long braids and this was a big event. Crea can still feel her daughter's silky tresses as she combed out the braids, lingering goodbye, and placed the scissors at her shoulder. "Here?" she queried carefully. Fair, archly studying herself in the mirror, took some time selecting exactly what length. Then Crea began, and a cinnamon pile of childhood lay forever gone at their feet. She has kept a strand of it, tied with ribbon, somewhere.

○

Fair doesn't know how long she's been in this room. She hasn't seen or heard a soul for countless hours, and the space is lit only by a crack under the door. She is naked and cold. There's no furniture, only a bowl for her toilet that already stinks. Food left for her is drying up on the tray; she has long ago drunk all the liquids. They certainly know what they're doing, she thinks. Even her agony of hunger is surpassed in desolation by the specter of nothingness around her. She holds close the image of her father's face smiling encouragement at her, remembers his smell, salty and musty. One day he had carried her in her sleep and she half woke at the motion. She grasps at and relives over and over that feeling of absolute trust and safety.

Someone opens the door and blinds her with light. Illuminates her pitiful crouch in the corner, arm over her eyes.

"Ha!" crackles Mme. J. "What a miserable little twit of a thing! You call that a female?"

"Now," says the doctor's hard gritty voice persuasively, "we're going to cooperate, aren't we?"

A man in uniform is grabbing Fair's arm and pulling her to her feet, twisting her arms behind her back.

"What do you have to say?" snaps the doctor. Fair doesn't answer. The doctor slaps her face. "What the devil is the matter with you? Do you want to die here?"

"You'll have to hurt her," urges Mme. J. from the shadows. "Want me to?"

The doctor squeezes Fair's chin tight, juts her warty face up close. "She doesn't need to be hurt, now does she? She knows she's all alone. We're all she has now. She'll be a good girl."

Fair jerks her chin up in response, bringing a glint of what could be called reluctant admiration into the doctor's eyes.

"Don't you know what will happen to you?" she yells. "Your parents don't know where you are, they can never find you. And they don't care, either. Listen to me. Madame Jacqueline's wand will be like nothing after you've had a taste of the baron and his pals. And they won't go easy on you either, the way you've behaved. I never saw such an insane suicidal idiot."

She steps back and gestures to the man to release Fair.

"Just you wait," crows Mme. J. "Oh, you've got it coming to you!"

Before they leave, fresh food is brought, hot and smelling delicious. On the new tray Fair finds water and tea and drinks them greedily. She doesn't touch the food but dozes fitfully beside it, breathing it in, dreaming distorted images of home. This time when she cries out to them, her parents turn their backs.

○

"Well," says the doctor to the baron a few days later, "she's probably going to die. We even stopped liquids and she still won't give in."

They are lounging after dinner in plush low-slung chairs on either side of a fireplace. The spacious ornate room used to be the central gathering place of the old lodge and still boasts the heads of animals on walls. The

baron is more than fat. He's in his lardish way grandiose, a very adver-
tisement for untamed flesh. He's wearing a purple silk jacket, part of his
royalty fancy. But in fact he never forgets he grew up Bobby Lemoyne on
the wrong side of Brooklyn, and made his first fortune in the 30s trafficking
in black market drinking water (some of it tainted, but who would tell?).

"She can't get away with it," he grunts. Takes a swig of brandy.

"Dying is one thing people do tend to get away with."

"Shit. I want to sell her back eventually. What'll we do?"

"Does it really matter? You've got another cargo of girls coming in this
week."

"Already?"

"One of them is the Randall child. She's only fourteen but they say the
boobs on her!" The Baron's bulk stirs greedily. "That'll keep you plenty
busy. Why not put pitiful little sour pussy to work in the kitchen?"

"I could have her gang raped. The boys would be grateful."

"She's a bag of bones. I don't think they would, frankly."

"Bitch."

"Who knows, when she stops being so dramatic and heroic maybe the
drudgery will change her mind. Maybe she'll come crawling to you after
all. And you'll have her first, the way you like it."

The baron loves this idea, as the doctor well knows.

And so it happens that the next day Fair's trance is broken by a crash.
She's on a concrete floor and her nose is bleeding. While she lies there,
who knows how long, she escapes home again in another dream so that
when she feels a warm presence, a nose breathing on hers, it must be
her father, come upstairs to make sure she's asleep. Then consciousness
breaks through and she's looking into the concerned chocolate eyes of a
half grown puppy black as coal. He cocks his head and gives an inquiring
whine.

"Hey," she whispers.

She manages to slowly sit up and give the dog a feeble embrace. He pa-
rades purposefully over to his water bowl and takes a drink. She follows on
her hands and knees, gulps musty water, sponges her throbbing nose.

"Raven!" squawks a voice. "Get over here!"

A thin young woman, maybe twenty, limp yellow hair twined with
feathers, stands over them, hands on hips.

"So," she snorts, "You steal from dogs now, do you?" She gives Fair a
nasty prod with her booted foot. "Beat it."

Fair crawls a short distance, followed by Raven.

"Raven, get the fuck over here, you turd! Leave be the garbage."

The woman has a slight southern accent, must be from the States.

"I'm from Massachusetts," Fair tries faintly.

"And I'm from the fucking moon."

Woman and dog are gone and Fair, alone again in cold darkness, wails for mercy.

○

Three weeks later Fair is hunched over a mound of dirty dishes, rescuing edible bits for stew for the slaves and scraping off the rest for Seth the dishwasher, a ruddy young man with fierce eyebrows. They wear the orange jumpsuits of all the lower-level staff, bright orange so they can always be spotted. The woman with the feathers hovers near urging haste.

Just before sunset, which now in April doesn't come until around nine o'clock, Fair is able to slip outside to the alleyway, sit for a little while in the last crimson glow of sky, arm around Raven, listening to Seth's harmonica. If the baron and his cohorts knew the nourishing simmer of joy these moments provide her, they would be appalled. She can live all day in grinding exhaustion just savoring the few minutes of this vast view, this loyal dog, this music, this ugly beauty of a man. Seth's features singly seem crude or displaced — flat nose, thin long lips, stiff black hair stuffed behind large ears, heavy shoulders — but the sum of him is magnetic. Though barely nineteen, he's been a solace for her, a harbor. He weaves for her old stories he heard from his Mohawk father who was killed as a young man trying to defend Native lands from clearcutting, and from his grandparents, swirling vivid sketches of times close to the earth. She can taste the thin frosted air, hear the bellow of bears, feel the curve of the silent canoe. Every once in a while Fair and Seth even manage to meet secretly, just before their rooms are locked for the night, in a storage room smelling of mildew and rust.

Seth is playing a melody she remembers. The nostalgic notes pierce to her soul. Beyond the kitchen compound the pine forest sweeps into the distance. On a topmost branch an owl squats belligerently, tufted head twirling. A hawk rides the air, wings motionless, dipping, soaring, surfing the currents, seeing how long it can go without moving a muscle. Beside her, Raven shifts to press closer. Seth stops, looking at Fair.

"You have music hands," he says. "Long fingers. Long fingers for such small hands."

She smiles at her hand looped in Raven's fur. "That's what my mom says. No piano here, though, at least not for us."

"I'll teach you the harmonica."

"At home I practiced piano every day. I'm going to forget everything!"

Seth shakes his head. They aren't supposed to talk about captivity in these precious free moments, they've agreed to that. His music begins again, for all answer.

A month later Mr. Simms shows up to collect his prize, an hour with a trained and docile Fair. Here he comes, wispy jaunty little Mr. Simms, all dressed up for his royal visit, his erotic fantasy. He is enraged when told Fair is not available. He insists. So they bring him, blindfolded, a grim scrawny creature he barely recognizes. Her magnificent red curls have been reduced to a scrappy cap, the crumpled orange overalls drape formlessly. She stands rigidly defiant, feet apart like a combatant, mouth set in a bull-dog jaw. They tell him he can do whatever he wants, but he only slaps her, halfheartedly. Then they give him Maeve instead.

On his way home, imagine how apoplectic Mr. Simms would be to know that the very same night, Fair's breasts are kissed for the first time not by bandits or goons or barons or wily piano teachers, but by a surly young nobody named Seth.

Episode 8

Keepers

"What did you just say?"

Fair turns towards the sharp voice, wants to retort, "I wasn't talking to you," but knows far better than that.

"My mother," she mumbles. "I was just mentioning my mother."

"Her name."

Fair does not want to repeat her mother's name to this person. She knows she must, but hesitates as long as she dares.

The bell rings. The mess hall clanks and creaks as everybody hastily scrapes last mouthfuls from tin plates and gets up from the long tables. Truth has put her booted foot on the bench so Fair can't rise. People recede around them. Even the feisty friend to whom Fair had been describing her home and family lingers only briefly. Fair with lowered head hears and feels that she's now alone with their dreaded supervisor. She takes a breath and looks up to meet the woman's eyes. But the expression she sees there is totally unexpected. Skinny snaky Truth, yellow hair decorated with her signature bluish feathers, looks astonished.

"Is her name Crea?"

"How do you know my mother's name?"

Now dread begins to pluck at Fair. Her mother abducted too? Was she searching for Fair after all, and they got hold of her somehow?

"Your grandmother's Tati. Tatyana."

Fair spits out, "What have you done with them?"

But Truth for once doesn't register her tone, or even her words.

"I know Tati," she says quietly. "She shot me."

Then she takes her foot off the bench and almost gently pulls Fair by the arm. They go up some stairs to an area Fair has never seen before, a room with desks and a big heavily shaded window, where they sit facing each other. In the old ski lodge this must have been a recreation area. On one side a giant three-sided fireplace and on the other a bar, now lined with electronic equipment.

"If I'd only known," says Truth. Her wild bony face has unbelievably softened. "She was good to me. I would've treated you better."

Through Fair's brain flash the hundreds of times over the last year and a half since she was brought here, when Truth has yelled at her, pushed her around, mocked her misery. Fair is confused and annoyed by her sudden humanity.

"Happened about five years ago," Truth pursues. "I was only fourteen. Our gang of teens had been on the road forever. Coming up from the south, from Durham, trying to get north like everybody else. I left my mama there, don't know why to this day. Mean of me. Poor mama. By the time we got all the way up there to Massachusetts we were so hungry, all we'd had to eat for days was rotten potatoes. And thirsty. We'd pass by water but we knew enough not to drink it. So here was this town, this swanky neighborhood. Grand houses. But nobody there any more except for Tati and them. Her man, and her dog Fox. As sweet a dog as ever you saw."

Truth stops. She swipes at her face, looks amazed at her own tears. Fair recalls her grandmother's little dog, a mutt with floppy ears, and kissing him goodbye when she and her parents were starting for Canada.

"Well, we wanted that dog to eat," Truth goes on implacably. "Everyone on the road was eating what they could get. So we attacked their car, to make them give him up. And your grandmother shot me. Got out this rifle, shot me in my leg. My so-called friends took off like wildfire. Left me there bleeding on the street. Your grandmother and him took care of me. Brought me with them all the way up to Burlington."

Truth stops and stares at some memory.

Fair clears her throat. "Wow," she ventures.

"Not the end of story. Wish it was. But the border closed and they couldn't get papers. So I ran away from them. And I took Fox. And I sold him."

"For food?"

"Dogmeat. Yep. Somebody had a foxy burger."

Truth breaks into her trademark cackle and then opens her mouth in a roaring sob.

Fair stands up and goes to the window, pulls back the blind. She has no impulse to comfort the bawling behind her. She brings her mind to focus on studying this view of the baron's compound. She and Seth have planned their escape in detail, but from here she can see obstacles and opportunities they didn't know about. As expected, the plan of the old ski lodge remains, picnic area planted with vegetables, lift huts turned tool sheds. But right down there in the glaring September sun there's a passage through from the kitchen yard they thought was blocked — all they can see from the stoop is the high kitchen fence. And beyond that, just before the barbed wire fence and thickly forested hills, is a deep trough like a moat they hadn't reckoned on at all.

Fair herself has stopped crying long ago. Something dried them up, her tears, she shed so many. For her father's death, her stepfather's despotism, her ordeal here, and imagining her poor mother's agony. Fair's not even sure she can feel her own heart any more, not even for Seth, it's that shriveled and out of touch, scudding elusively somewhere far back in the cavity of her chest.

She turns back to gaze down at her blubbering tormentor.

"Too bad," she intones ironically.

$\bigcirc$

That night she tells Seth, "I couldn't see where the moat ends. Maybe it goes all the way around."

"Damn, that's where we planned to cross."

Crouched in darkness in the third-floor storage closet, they have hardly half an hour before their dorms are locked for the night. Hemmed in by mops and pails, assailed with moldy odors, they subsist on this secret sanctuary where they manage to meet almost every week, making love as best they can on a layer of musty rugs. Over time they've crafted an opening in the wall where they keep some dark clothes, their escape in mind. All they have to do before they make a run for it is stash a supply of food and water.

"But we still have to go by the north gate," he adds, "and we should make our move soon."

"Okay, then what about the 20th, when the baron's having that big harvest feast?"

"Good idea." Seth accentuates his approval with a hug. "Let's go over the plan. So. We wait here in the closet while the compound settles down for the night, then we sneak out."

"Wait, first we lose the overalls, put on dark clothes."

"Right…so then we maneuver down to the second floor where we can drop from the window. Has to be close to midnight, just before the sleepy evening guards get replaced. They'll be bleary by then."

"And if we get separated, we'll meet in the forest up there at the highest fire tower."

Every detail has been etched out in these precious minutes while they hold each other close.

But it does not happen like that at all.

A few weeks after Truth's transforming revelation, Fair has just slipped into the storage closet, waiting for Seth. She has managed to ferret a canteen of water from the kitchen, stuff it in the wall crevice. She crouches in the dark starting to warm in anticipation. He will open and shut the door in a flash and fall on his knees to engulf her.

But suddenly she hears a drumming commotion, growing. It's a few seconds before she recognizes the thudding of feet. Yells, screams, sirens. Her impulse to bolt is staved off by knowing she'll miss Seth. As a result, when she finally does peer out, the hallway is deserted, the whole floor is deserted, and through the windows comes a wild orange glow that can only be fire. Without one thought, she grabs dark trousers and the canteen, dashes down the two flights of stairs right out the front door. While she heads toward the flaming forest following their plan, everyone else is fleeing in the other direction. Abruptly someone stops dead in front of her. Blocking her way is Truth.

For a split second they stare at each other, unmoving. Their faces glint and change shape in the firelight. Shouts, an explosion, feet tramping, alarms blaring, bodies bumping frantically into them, yelling and shoving. Then Truth pulls from her belt a hefty gleaming knife. Fair braces. Should she fight? Does she have a chance? Truth steps closer.

"Take this," she mutters. She holds the knife out to Fair. "Turn back and take a left."

Fair grabs the knife, takes one last flabbergasted look at Truth, and swirls around taking off like a deer. When she finally stops, her breath slicing her lungs, she's looking at a stack of bicycles, the bike repair shop. She drops the telltale orange overalls, pulls on the dark pants, rifles through the stack for a bike that works, and speeds off, joining the crowd streaming toward the front gates. Just as she passes through, she turns her head in time to see other slaves who briefly tasted freedom, getting rounded up and herded back. She swerves off the road into the woods, following a dusty path until it ends in nowhere, and keeps going.

Hours later, having abandoned the bike and flailed through underbrush that scratches at her arms, she drops like a stone to a mossy hillock, knowing she's reached her limit. Fighting for breath, terror gradually receding to make way for thought, she now fully realizes she has left Seth behind. Not only that, in the unlikely event he too escaped, she's been running in the opposite direction from the fire tower, their emergency meeting place. She groans for the loss of him, but sorrow loses out to exhaustion in sleep.

Toward dawn she wakes at a mounting sound, something tearing nearer through the underbrush. Is it the baron's goons? Or if it's the Guards, are they on the baron's take or loyal to her stepfather? Shrinking into the smallest possible embryo shape, she slowly extracts the knife and waits for the assault. But what she sees leaping at her is the beloved black shape of Raven the dog. He grins and pants, dances, pummels himself into her. For an icy instant she fears he's been followed. She listens. Has he brought them with him? But outside his snuffles and joy whines, the only sound is birdsong.

○

On this same morning, Fair's mother Crea swims up from sleep to a split second of peace, before her child's fate clutches at her once more. As usual, though she concentrates hard to remember the feel of that brief moment, the only rest she ever knows, it wafts mercilessly away. Her hus-

band's weight is pressed against her and she'll have to disturb him to move,
so she rigidly waits.

A few hours later he comes to the doorway of Fair's room, where Crea is
sitting on the bed, just sitting, as always.

"The news is pretty bad from the Ontario front," he says. He's in uniform on his way out. "I may have to be gone for a few days."

She tries to look interested. "Leaving now? Will you be back by
Saturday?"

"Oh, I expect so. Count me in for the mayor's dinner."

Vaguely she wonders if he's going off on another tryst with his mistress
or whether the skirmishes over the diversion of the Ottawa River have really worsened that much.

They look at each other briefly in silence. General Hanley still carries
his middle years with arrogant aplomb. White hair clipped close to noble
head, tall broad-shouldered frame quick footed. But Crea, though barely
over forty, has gained a pound for every month her daughter's been missing
and her once beautiful face has rounded to dough. She's as slumped and
limp as an invalid. Han's scorn shows in his face.

In the afternoon Crea goes to visit Fleur.

The limousine crosses the bridge and lets Crea off half way up the next
hill. She waits until it's out of sight, looking back out at Lake Massawippi.
Though wilted to reveal yards of dry caked mud, the lake sparkles soothingly in the glaring autumn sun. Crea no longer dares to ride her bike;
it's too dangerous. Desperate illegal American immigrants crossing the
border have made Petit Chapeau a through point on their way north, escaping the deadly heat, chaos, and disease engulfing the U.S. She knows
that many of these shacks she's now approaching hide people in fear for
their lives. Forged papers are common, but if the Americans are caught,
though sometimes deported, usually they are shot at once. The path to the
cluster of shacks too is cracked mud from the alternate violent floods and
droughts.

As soon as she steps into the little room, she can see that Fleur is even
worse today. Her wizened old face is all eyes, frightened black pools in
yellowish puckers. She has shrunk under the gray blanket to the size of a
child. She raises her hand for Crea's grasp. The hand is cold and dry, mere
bone.

"So happy you came."

"Of course, Fleur dear, it's Thursday. I always come on Thursdays."

Crea pulls a chair closer, sits heavily into the sense of release. Here she
won't be judged. Her husband won't deride her, her own servants won't
stare in pity or contempt. She will feel love, loved and loving. She kisses
Fleur's chalky forehead, caresses her hand.

"Warm," murmurs Fleur.

"I brought you some milk and fresh fruit. Would you like them now?"

"Thank you. I don't want anything today. I'm going soon and I need to tell you something." Her raspy soft voice the nasal French Canadian sing-song. "Remember when we met? By my house that you live in? That they took from me and my poor Bernard?"

"Of course I remember. Do you want me to tell you about the house? The old oak is doing fine…"

"No, no." Fleur begins to get excited, calling on all her strength. "Listen to me, please. Ecoute, mon enfant. Fleur is going to tell you a truth that I know you do not wish to hear. I hesitate to upset you. But my time is very short. Listen. You must go in search of your daughter."

Crea sighs, indulgent. "You know I can't."

"Why, why? This time you must listen. I am sorry to tell you, my magnificent friend, but you are dying like me. You used to be so very beautiful, and so strong a body. My curse on my house where you live has happened. You are suffering, miserable, decaying. Your child that you adore has been taken, you have no hope or joy. You are not alive!"

Crea anxiously tries to pull her hand away but Fleur will not let go.

"Fleur no, don't say those things…"

"Because I care about you, because it is my curse that did this, you must do as I say. I demand it with my last breaths. Oh, if I could give you my courage!"

"But you know I can't do it."

This time Fleur is silent, black eyes pulling her in.

"Can't," Crea repeats mechanically. "Han would follow me, punish me. I don't know where Fair is, I have no idea. Reports say to the west of Montreal, but where? That's huge territory. We know it's probably one of the barons, but which one? So you see…anyway, Han's troops are looking all the time, they'll find her soon, he says so."

She forces her hand away, gets up and steps back from the bed. But the black pools hold her firm.

"Marcel came to visit me," Fleur finally says. "He will help you."

"Why? Why should he help me? He's married now."

"Come, come. Don't argue. First of all he and his wife are separated, didn't you know that? And besides he's in big trouble from his actions against the Zorians, that religious cult. You've heard about that?"

"How can it be illegal to think Zoria's a fake? She claims she's pregnant with Jesus! How ridiculous can you…besides, Marcel has his business to attend to, he can't just…he's not going anywhere."

But Crea's dismissal is weakened by a pressing image of Marcel, his urgent face coming close that one time he kissed her, his mouth. Marcel alone again, not living with his wife! Old emotions press her chest.

It's been five years now since she and Marcel stopped falling in love, but it seems a forever time. Han's grimly amused confrontation, tossing his knowledge of her trysts at her, making it clear that nothing she ever did was a secret from him, had meant an end to the joy of Marcel. Sure, she'd been a coward, but she at least credits herself with wanting most to protect him from what Han could too clearly do to him. Marcel had never understood. He went ahead and got married, and long afterwards every time he saw Crea he gave her a sullen wounded frown, a sad clown face that sliced her heart.

"It's not healthy to say out loud that Zoria is a fake," Fleur countered. "One can think whatever one wants, but Marcel and his people are noisy about it. He's never been a favorite with the authorities anyway. He's angry and he's a leader. They don't like that."

"No, they don't," Crea agrees reluctantly. "You're right that Zoria's cult is good for keeping people in line. And I'm sure Han would love to make trouble for Marcel."

"So," Fleur quavers triumphantly, "you see he's got to leave town anyway!"

◯

In the forest Fair has discerned the rising sun through a gray blanket of sky. Over in the opposite direction, which must be west, dark fumes in the far distance still waft from the baron's compound. She has shared some water with Raven, he lies solidly asleep beside her. All her impulses cry start running again, but her reeling brain stalls, wants a plan. Keep going east? Must find soldiers loyal to General Hanley. Go south? Petit Chapeau is probably southward. Stay deep in the forest, don't risk people. The baron will soon alert everyone to look out for her. At least she's no longer wearing orange. But will he figure out that Raven could be with her? Tell them to look for a black dog and a red haired girl? Pretty conspicuous. Will he be grilling Seth? Hurting Seth? But at least, if Seth is still captive, he'll know she's escaped, will exult no matter what.

She heads southeast.

Two days later, while Fair and Raven are emerging from the woods to a vast view of the churning St. Lawrence River, Crea comes into Marcel's shop. He nods to her formally, continuing discussion of a clock repair with a customer. She turns to look back at the street, drawing deep breaths to keep from rushing out again. She barely sees the faces passing by, the ripple of the lake.

Why am I here? She panics. This is hopeless, insane, dangerous. But Fleur's admonishment has unaccountably stirred her. Just taking an action like this, actually coming into Marcel's shop for such a purpose, has given her a flash of excitement that's so unfamiliar she thinks for an instant she must be ill. She looks at him aslant, pretending to examine a mended espresso pot. His dark hair is ridged with gray but otherwise it falls across his forehead exactly as it used to. Will he really help her? The very idea that she herself could set out to look for Fair, could try to escape from Han, feels like stepping off a cliff.

Just as Marcel comes to stand beside Crea, says, "You came. Fleur said you would," Fair is clambering down the dry stony slope to the river's edge. Wind starts from somewhere, whips up waves, chills Fair's face. Raven laps water as she shades her eyes to study a boat docked less than half a mile away. It looks like a military craft, and sure enough she spots the gray-blue uniforms of the Guards. This is what she's been hoping for, to get to the Guards loyal to her stepfather without any intermediaries who might betray her. In the forest she avoided several groups who might have helped, even illegal American immigrants clearly on the run, for fear they would turn her over to the baron.

Exhaustion and hunger fog Fair's perceptions. Raven has caught and devoured small creatures as he could, but she has subsisted on berries and roots. In her dizziness the boat and its crew appear mystical, heroic. As she hurries toward them, she thinks of her mother, how stunned with joy she will be, how it will feel to hold each other again.

Her mother in this moment meets Marcel's eyes. There she no longer sees the passion of old days, but still deep caring. She replies, "Fleur did persuade me. She says you want to help me find Fair."

"Come on, let's go inside," he says, putting an arm around her shoulders, guiding her to the back of the shop, through the doorway to his home. It's as she remembers, spare, crowded, shabby. There's the same old couch and table, potbellied stove, rows of mismatched dishes. He hands her coffee without asking.

"I've had a solid report," he says. "Trustworthy. Fair is being held by a baron somewhere northeast of Montreal."

"But Han thinks she's near Toronto, the opposite direction."

The look of pity on Marcel's face brings her a stab of fury at Han, stab like a shot of energy. "Of course, he's been lying," she adds quickly, realizing only as she says it that it's true.

As she sips at the coffee, the heat of it joins with her anger. She feels strong. She smiles tightly, straightens her shoulders.

Late the next morning Fair is lying sleepily in a luxurious bed in the Baie St. Paul Hotel, clean, well fed, well clothed, and well guarded. Outside, a buffeted rain is all that's left of the hurricane that raged all evening and into the night. The storm made eview contact so sporadic, they have not yet been able to reach her mother. General Hanley, however, is reported to be on his way himself to take her home. Raven is curled up beside the bed on the plush plum-colored carpet.

A cursory knock, and in strides Lieutenant Renaud, her stepfather's friend whom she has remembered from his many visits to their house in Petit Chapeau. He offers up more predictable murmurs about how she's grown, she's now a woman, amazing, and thanks to God for her safety, and much about miracles. He's a hefty, slick haired, weasel nosed man, but to Fair living proof that truly everything is now going to be all right. She smiles and inches up a bit on the pillow.

"I'm being lazy," she apologizes.

Crea and Marcel have been traveling since before dawn, their horse-drawn wagon shaken continuously by the storm's last winds. Now, in a town near Trois-Rivières they're climbing down from the back of the wagon, stepping over rivers of mud. Crea has dyed her blond hair brown, and though a few of her elegant clothes are pressed into her backpack, she wears the frayed outfit of a laborer. Marcel hasn't shaved, planning a beard for disguise, and they make a grubby looking pair. The woman who shows them their tiny room in the attic of her house is casual to the point of rude. As Marcel puts a week's rent in cash into her outstretched palm, she comments, "You won't find much work around here."

The room is quite clean and pretty though, and as soon as the door closes they fall exhausted onto the bed to sleep. When Crea again opens her eyes, the gray light slanting through the little window is dimming towards dusk. She lies very still, listening to her heart soar and scream, elated and terrified at what she has done. She expects Han to walk in the door any minute, laugh at her, cart Marcel off to an unpleasant death, and drag her humiliated back to her wifely prison.

She forces herself to calm in picturing him, some place in Ontario or wherever, pacing the floor, grinding his teeth, impotent. Servants watching her probably will have reported her tardiness by yesterday evening. They will have first thought she was simply late, remiss in her duties, which already involved some punishable breach. Then later Han probably gave an order to look for her discreetly. Finally, sometime after midnight he will have caught the first real alarm, told his spies to look in her closet, her desk. They will have found enough things missing to get the picture. Has he thought of checking on Marcel? No doubt. She sees Guards break-ing down the door to Marcel's shop. Han's final flash of indignity: the knowledge they are together. He'll send out bulletins about her flying in all directions, but how will he phrase them without bringing embarrass-ment on himself?

Crea turns her head to look at Marcel's profile. The long black lashes of his closed eyes, his mouth slightly open, his hands laced together on his chest, like a prayer. Could she begin to love him again? Desire has not intruded on her misery for years, she can't even remember what it feels like. Sex now means only the persistent commands and thrustings of Han, often bruising her just for his fun. She can't believe she'll never be subjected to Han again. All she asks is to find Fair. That's the only future she dares.

Fair this afternoon takes a walk around the hotel, Raven at her heels. She stops in a spacious lounge to look out the window at the fog-blurred grounds and river beyond. In the aftermath of the storm broken tree branches are strewn about amid bits of unidentifiable objects, here and there a hat, a plank, a wheel, even a fully-formed little roof blown over from somewhere that stands by itself in the streaming mud.

But the rain is hardly more than mist now, and she has high hopes that she'll be on the eview with her mother soon. Lieutenant Renaud promised her this morning that the system would surely be up sometime today. Then as she passes by the reception desk in the main lobby, she sees a row of screens all working perfectly well.

Before she can process her annoyance that no one has told her, she catches sight of a full-screen image of her mother's face. Across it words blare, "Missing! Reward!" She continues walking past, simply because her frozen brain can't catch up with the knowledge.

Keeping a casual stroll, masking her expression in mild meditation, even pausing now and then to pretend interest in something, her slave's instincts return in sickening force. If her mother is missing and they have not told her, it can mean anything. This haven is now ablaze with deception, danger.

Back in her room, Fair finds her canteen and the knife Truth gave her, stuffs them into one of the fancy bags that her new clothes were delivered in. Raven circles and whines, asking what's wrong. Outside the light is fading towards dusk. Think, think. So far they have no idea that she knows, have no reason to imagine she'll try escape. But soon they'll be wondering why she hasn't asked to connect to the eview — they must be preparing for that confrontation any time now. She ties a scarf over her telltale hair and heads for the staff exit.

In their attic room, Crea is changing her clothes while Marcel is down the hall in the bathroom. They've rigged up a clothesline of sorts, stretched across from bed to window, where their shabby outfits dangle damply. She hopes that the pleated dress she has chosen is humble enough for her supposed status. The automatic rituals of daily life anchor her. She begins to sense hope, hope and energy, long lost. While Fair and Raven are hurrying down the back staircase of the hotel, Crea turns to greet Marcel.

Episode 9

Directions

Marcel is standing very close to Crea, but she doesn't move away even though acutely aware that she's naked under the robe. They remain like this much longer than they need to, looking out the window of their fourth-floor room on St. Hubert.

"The first snow and it's January," he says. "Mon pays c'est l'hiver."

"My country is winter?"

"An old ballad. It used to be true."

Crea has just washed and her wet hair is swathed in a towel. Out in the gray street from a gray sky float little bleached snow ornaments spotting and starting to mantle the gray roofs, steps, and railings of the battered old Montreal town houses. People stop in their hurry and gaze upwards, on their faces nostalgia and apprehension. A child is laughing, tugging at his mother's hand in a squirm, tongue outstretched to catch a fleeting sparkle. He's wearing a long red stocking cap, too big, with the tail wrapped around his neck.

"Shall we go out early?" Marcel's voice is light. "It could melt later."

"Yes," she replies, trying to match his tone. She does not say, "I wonder if it's snowing wherever she is." No point in clouding his small joy.

Their search for Fair has so far been fruitless, one false lead after another. But Montreal's library has public access to the internet, and later that day they will meet with yet another person who is said to know something.

When they fled Petit Chapeau four months ago, Marcel had said, "We might have to stay in the same room most of the time, but now that we're just good friends, I think we can manage, don't you?" "

She'd responded gratefully, "Of course, thanks, I'm glad that's clear."

She was awkward and careful those first weeks on the road, as they learned the deft complexities of avoiding intimacy in close quarters. Here, although the room is small, they've pushed the two single beds up against opposite walls, hung chairs with clothes as at least symbolic barriers. There's a table near the window designated common space, where they share meals or read or just talk over coffee or wine. By sheer will and self-conscious connivance they've managed to live quite comfortably as the brother and sister they tell strangers they are.

But it's getting harder. They too much enjoy being together. Even with his meetings and her research, they choose to spend their extra time in each other's company. Crea has lost the fat accumulated in her despair; her face no longer looks bloated. The clothes she brought have to be belted so as not to droop. She sees the change in Marcel's eyes, and in the reactions of other men. She knows she has become beautiful again.

She shivers and he says, "I'll go down to the bathroom so you can get dressed. You're cold." She turns to look up at him and he adds, "Your hair covered like that, I forget you're a brunette now." He's beaming but trying to make his admiration brotherly. "Someday, soon I hope, you can be blond again."

"And you can shave off that bush of a beard!" she laughs.

As they set out for the library the snow has gathered enough to coat the sidewalks, crunch under their boots.

"Was it March last year when it snowed?"

"I think so," he ponders, "yes, because remember we'd had all that rain? So we were just hoping it would stay frozen for a while because of the flooding." He goes on in submerged anger, "You were still there living with him."

Crea pats his shoulder soothingly, but stung. Won't he ever stop galling her with her humiliation? Instead of going on to apologize once again, she says pointedly, "I'm trying not to remember that."

"Sorry."

"Let's take the long route, it's so beautiful."

Passing through the Latin Quarter, they stroll down St. Catherine Street, where snow is whitening everything to freshness, the broken, neglected, and discarded quietly taking on soft shapes. Crea and Marcel clear a space on a bench inside the McGill campus, now used for military drills and administration because all student age people are serving in the Guards. But some teenagers are throwing snowballs and rolling in the snow in mock death throes, young cheeks red and laughter ringing. There are still big old trees here, oaks and hardy pines, branches sleeved in white lace. Marcel's beard has grown icelets, and Crea smoothes them away. For this little while it's as if the world were whole again.

Leaving her in the library tracking barons on the internet, Marcel heads for his meeting. His group of activists, the Credos, are increasingly frowned upon by the public as well as officials. Canada has become fertile ground for the Zorians by this time. Late in 2048, Zoria had finally achieved a mass rally in Toronto like the ones she'd been holding in the U.S. for several years. It was a great success. People screamed and fainted, and in the frenzy some were trampled underfoot and seriously hurt. Many were converted. But now there's been a development in doctrine. It's no longer enough to declare faith in the coming of Jesus from the womb of Zoria, to confess your sins, and to donate your money and valuables. Now you must recognize that males have a more direct route to God. Females who want to join the chosen and assure their entry to Heaven are exhorted to confirm their sanctity by mating with a male Zorian.

"It's rape," Linette rails whenever she gets the chance. One of the Credo leaders, Linette is stout and feisty and fearless. She stands on street

corners proclaiming Zoria a fake, denouncing the four years of required
military service, and the government's increasing disarray and despotism.
She's been arrested more than once.

"Needless to say," Linette likes to mock, "the new religion is suddenly
very popular with men. They all can't wait to convert the girls."

As Marcel rounds the corner approaching the church where the Credos
are to meet, he stops short. At the top of the steps stand two Guards with
machine guns. Quickly, without looking again, Marcel crosses the street
and heads the other way. Fortunately, the Credos have foreseen this pos-
sibility. The alternative meeting place is a mile west, near Atwater, in a
warehouse used to store old machinery.

When he arrives, the meeting is just getting started. Smiles and high
fives signal satisfaction at the successful ruse. But there's a nervous tension
in the air with the realization that officials have taken a new step in efforts
to obstruct them.

Linette is introducing the speaker, a lanky young man from
Newfoundland named Miro. He's the person Marcel and Crea are to meet
with that afternoon because he reportedly has some news about Fair.

"In St. John's we're looking to Montreal to consolidate our progress,"
Miro tells them. His voice is deep and quiet. He moves his long hands
over the air around him as if including it in his plea. "We have thousands
of citizens joining us, and the pockets of Credos in the U.S. are growing
stronger. This is great progress, given that the current outbreak of ebola
there is being blamed on us, as unbelievers. You know the logic — our
heresy angers God, so he sends disasters to punish us. Unfortunately, this
slander means polarization is growing too. We may have some confron-
tations on our hands, and we need to prepare for that. I know we are
peaceful people, but these are not peaceful times."

Miro is a good speaker, and Marcel admires his method of balancing
calm logic with forcefulness. Afterwards, Linette introduces them to each
other. The three of them stand for some time in the shadow of a rusted-
out steamroller, unable to stop discussing strategy, shared outrage a balm.
Marcel likes Linette. It's not only her fiery courage, it's her soft chin and
small teeth, and the way she stands with her feet apart, like a little boxer.

Marcel and Miro set out for St. Hubert Street around three o'clock.
The snow has stopped. It's still cold enough to keep the city whitely
dusted and draped, drifts quickly graying with soot. The coal-fired plants
have been shut down, but not yet all the incinerators, so the polluted air
keeps coming. The sounds along St. Catherine Street are muted — horses'
hooves, bicycles, tramping feet, the occasional motor of a Guard convoy.
Some people have crafted sleighs for their horses out of wagons with skis
or planed planks attached. The sky is slate and already dimming to evening.

Crea has opened wine and lit a candle, and she greets Miro with a glowing intensity that makes it hard for either man to concentrate in a businesslike way. Watching the effect she has on Miro has Marcel confounded with unexpected jealousy and a sudden painful recognition of his own desire, like a blow to the stomach. Up until this moment he had truly believed that the love for her he had once begun to feel, almost six years ago, was past and done with, replaced with admirable and steadfast friendship. Now, at the table drinking wine and eating bread with cheese and talking politics, noting the astonished admiration in Miro's face, gazing at her Marcel feels such a hot stab of lust that he nearly groans out loud.

Crea's heavy breasts are wrapped in a dark turtleneck sweater, moving as she moves, caressing his eyes. Watching the fine soft slant of her profile, the warming gestures of her slim hands, the curve of her hip, the quick and blazing smile of her generous mouth, he feels as if he's drawing in more breath than he can hold. Marcel is normally ruled by his fury at the greed and corruption that has so damaged the earth and brought about tyranny in Canada. His crusade fills his soul. He has no room for this passion too much like love that suddenly suffocates him, but his body and heart are wilding against reason.

"Now," Crea says to Miro because she can't wait any longer, taking an extra sip of wine to calm herself, "please tell us what you know about my daughter."

○

At this moment, close to five o'clock on January 18, 2049, Fair Franklin has just crossed the border into Maine, although she doesn't know it yet. Because of clouds she lost her sense of direction two days ago, but had to keep moving because of the recruiters. They had spotted her when she stopped at a small farm to work for food.

"Your papers."

The men were her age, not yet twenty, and clearly enjoyed her trembling.

"I'm sorry, sir, I don't have any yet. I'm just trying to get home."

"Where have you been and where is home? Why aren't you in the service?"

Her lies got entangled and they told her not to move and went to call in the name she'd given them. She took some steps backward out of the searchlight, around the corner of the barn, and took off in pitch black through an orchard, Raven at her heels. At least they had not suspected that she's the general's stepdaughter, only saw her as a draft dodger to be punished and enlisted.

After two cold nights on the run, Fair is close to exhaustion and feels a fever coming on. The thought of sickness brings near panic. Snow turns to rain as she rests under the shelter of a rocky ledge, and she decides to stay here for the night. She digs a nest into the dirt, watches Raven run off to hunt. He returns with an offering for her, a mangled rabbit, but as usual she can't bear to eat it.

In the morning, she opens her eyes to see a road almost directly in front of her. We must get away from here, she thinks vaguely, but she can't move. Her head is burning. Her canteen is empty. For the first time since she was abducted, Fair gives up. She goes willingly into final feverish dreams where she and her father and mother and Seth all float together.

Some time that day, or maybe the next, she wakes from her stupor of fire and ice to hear voices nearby.

"I told you this would happen, Ma. Now are you satisfied?"

"It's a small world."

"Stop saying that. Haven't you got anything else to say?"

"It's a small world, certainly."

"Oh, for God's sake."

Through the trees appears a boy about thirteen leading a farm horse dragging a lopsided wagon. He parks them not ten feet from Fair, and starts inspecting a broken wheel. Behind him patters a pretty little woman with a purple umbrella. She looks quite unconcerned and more interested in their surroundings than in her son's dismay.

"It's a small world," she sings approvingly.

"Shut up, Ma. This is going to take forever to repair, you know. We can't leave our stuff. Could you at least get some firewood out of the back for God's sake?"

But the woman gazes about her with pleasure, as if they've just arrived for a picnic or a day at the beach. So the boy starts making a fire, grumbling and groaning.

"Damn stupid idea, anyway. They'll never let us cross the border. We should have stayed in Ashland. They would've figured out a way to get those toxins out of the soil, yeah, bet they already have. Just because you have a cousin in Saint whatever, doesn't mean a thing. They kill people trying to go there, it's a crazy idea. You're crazy. How did I ever get so unlucky, this is a number one disaster."

Flames are soon shooting up and while warming his hands he suddenly catches sight of Raven, who has crept out and is yearning towards the fire.

"Hey! Look Ma, a dog!"

Ma looks around confused, and smiles tenderly at her son. He holds out his hand to Raven, who sniffs it and moves closer. The boy pats him. After a while, Raven goes back into the shelter and grabs what's left of the rabbit and places it at his feet.

"Wow, how about that, ma. Dinner!"

He sets about cooking it with rudimentary haste. The smell of the roasting meat revives Fair to hunger. Raven starts barking and running back and forth from the fire to her, while the boy watches in puzzlement for a time. Then, because clearly he knows dogs, he gets the message. He looks under the ledge, and meets Fair's groggy half-closed eyes.

○

Crea is inflamed with Miro's news.

He has told them that Fair escaped Baron Lemoyne's compound during a fire, and eluded the Guards trying to take her to Han. For the first time, Crea and Marcel have details of what they've only heard rumored. Miro's specifics end with Baie St. Paul, however. After that there's only one vague report that she's been spotted heading east.

"Why would she go east?" Crea puzzles.

"She probably knows you're not in Petit Chapeau any more," Marcel speculates. "I'll bet she's even seen the wanted posters of you."

"But still. Everybody else is going north."

"Maybe that's why. Or maybe she doesn't have a choice, she's only going wherever as fast as she can."

Miro says, "I would bet she doesn't trust anybody now. She just has to travel. She's probably feeling pretty desperate."

Crea pictures Fair as last she saw her, at fifteen glowing pink and saucy, her now terrified and hunted child. Crea's fists clutch her belly and she says in a strange voice, "We're in the wrong place. We've got to go right now."

As soon as Miro leaves she starts to pack her few belongings, her heart so tight she feels it cracking. On her bed she's making neat little piles. Marcel watches her from the candle glow of the table. She's wearing a fine green skirt she brought from home, wrapped almost twice around her and belted. It drapes her more alluringly than well-fitting clothes ever could. She moves like the ocean.

Marcel says, "She's free. That's what matters."

"We're in the wrong place," she repeats.

"We can't leave now. We can't leave until I've helped Miro. It's absolutely crucial."

She turns to look at him. She's trying to smile. "You do what you need to do, and I will too."

Marcel jumps up and goes over to put an arm around her, sits her down on the bed.

"Crea, listen."

Her beautiful face is too close, is too distant. He embraces her fully, mouth on mouth.

Crea enters for an instant the luscious lie of passion. At last, at last. She has wanted him so much without quite knowing it. She returns his kisses, starts down into the heating spiral. But she hears "no" on her lips, and listens to it.

When she pulls away, sees his face crumpled with longing, she knows that she will not do this. Sex will not rule her again. She will not be duped again by desire. She speaks cold words to him, sends him riddled with shame away.

In the morning he leaves early, and only says, "I hope you change your mind."

When Linette invites him to her place for lunch, in a stupor he goes. He does everything she wants, this plump little fireball, and in her arms he finds some solace for a while. Only once, when her avid mouth is between his legs, does he imagine in spite of himself that it's Crea nursing at him instead, loving him.

By that time, Crea is on the road, walking east.

○

"Wheel's fixed, it's time to get going again," Miles says to Fair a few days later after supper. "First thing in the morning. You can ride in the wagon with Ma."

"And make you walk? No way," Fair insists. "I'm ok now."

Miles grins across the campfire with his childish diffidence and his mannish shrug. His round face is freely freckled. "You sure were a mess."

Fair pulls over the sleeping bag they've lent her, unrolls it, slips in, and snuggles down. "My savior," she grins back.

"Tell Ma to get in the sack."

"Come on, Iris," Fair obliges, "it's bedtime. I'll tell a story if you get in your bed."

Iris, sitting on a rock with a cup of cocoa, replies earnestly, "It's a small world."

"True, true," Fair responds. "Hey Miles, thanks for finding the mushrooms, they were yummy with the dandelion greens."

"So it's settled, right? We're going back to Ashland?"

"At least we're not going to try to get into Canada."

"No, that would be suicide for you, and they'd never let us in anyway. That's obvious."

Iris chirps, "It's a small world."

"It's been very hard for her," Miles apologizes. "She stopped talking to me almost as soon as we left home. It's like she doesn't want to be in reality."

"I don't blame her. At least you have her with you. I don't know if I'll ever see my mother again. If only I could at least tell her I'm ok…but I don't even know where she is!"

Miles looks anxious at her tone, pleads, "Just don't cry."

"Small, small world," Iris croons, getting into her sleeping bag.

"Thank you, Iris," says Fair.

"The story about the forest fire and escaping," requests Miles, adjusting the logs to a glow.

The three sleeping bags surround the hissing embers under the black net of tree limbs, a cold half moon. The blanketed horse shuffles close by. Raven is curled up on top of Fair's feet and Miles reaches out to throw a coat over him.

"Thanks, Miles. Say, why don't you tell a story this time?"

"How about when I was ten and I made a boat? Because of the flood."

"That would be a good one. Yes, please."

His voice is a husky rasp that has not yet changed into a man's. Sometimes when he relates exciting moments, it rises to a soprano again. Fair listens to the tale, harrowing but comforting too. To herself she says a prayer begging for her mother's safety, and then Seth's, and falls asleep imagining his arms around her.

◯

Crea is cornered. The young Guard was waiting for her when she came out of the bathroom in the wayside restaurant. A dilapidated shack, how could she have guessed a Guard would bother with such a place? How did he recognize her? He has pushed her up against the wall.

"You're under arrest, Mrs. Hanley."

"No, I'm sorry, my name is…"

"Zip it. Come with me."

He twists her arm behind her and leads her out the door, into a waiting jeep. He sits in the back with her, tells the driver to move on.

"Well," he says, "this is a lovely surprise. I can't believe you've avoided us all these months. And," he adds quietly, turning towards her to peer more closely, "you are as gorgeous as they say. You look a lot better than the photos. You are really something."

She keeps her eyes on the road grimly.

"My name is Lieutenant Pamiris, Stavos Pamiris. I know your husband. A fine man. A famous and fearless leader." His tone is not pandering or threatening but has an edge of irony. "He will be thrilled to hear you're coming home."

Before dusk the convoy stops, he and the driver get out for a while, and then the convoy moves on. Soon the jeep turns off onto a rutted driveway through a wooded area and stops in front of a small cabin. The lieutenant lights some lamps while his driver starts a fire. Then the driver salutes and drives away. Crea stands rigidly, already knowing what will come next.

"Now," says Stavos, "let's be friends. You know, if you please me, I may not have to contact your husband at all. You may just manage to escape. All it will cost you is a little fun."

Crea clutches her fists at her sides and says, "Never."

"Don't play the heroine. It's up to you. Anyway, let's have something to eat. Can you cook?" He starts unpacking bags of groceries, brings out a bottle of whiskey. "There's a shower upstairs. I won't bother you. Stavos never needs to force a woman."

Crea doesn't move. Her mind tumbles, falling over itself clutching at options. He's a good-looking man, probably not yet thirty, black hair and moustache, middle height with an exotic graceful carriage that belies his uniform. His self-confidence, his self-love, is repellent and intriguing. Could he be telling the truth?

"I want to find my daughter," she says. Try for his sympathy first.

She steps closer, just on the other side of the table. He stops moving, with a bunch of greens in his hand, watching her body.

"I haven't seen her for almost two years," she pursues. "She's seventeen now. I've missed two birthdays! Can you imagine a mother's grief? Imagine your own mother, how she would feel." Warming to her plea, Crea leans across the table, holds his eyes with hers. "Please let me go. I must find her, don't you see?"

Stavos puts down the greens and picks up the whiskey bottle, pours two glasses.

"Of course, sure. Crea. Have a drink, Crea my dear."

She sits down abruptly, hands to face, horrified to feel tears. He startles her by kneeling at her feet, hands on her shoulders.

"Crying doesn't work with me," he says. "Come on, buck up, it's not so bad. I'll make you happy, I promise. Stavos always makes his women happy." His breath smells of whiskey, his fingers stroking her neck are hot. He presses his groin against her knees. "Come on," he says softly, "we're going to take a shower."

He's pulling on her hand but she won't budge. So he grabs her by the waist and lifts her bodily off the chair. She starts with her fists but then he is bruising her arms, so she simply mutters, "This is force, this is force," while letting him lead her up the stairs.

Naked and erect, he watches her slowly undress. Hot water steams the room. Crea has not seen a shower since leaving home, and she cringes at this reminiscence of Han. Why is she doomed to be exploited and shamed like this? She does not resist again, while he soaps her, makes her soap him.

He lays her out on the bed, arranging her limbs like an art exhibit. The room is chilly but the bed warm and soft. He stands gazing at her, murmuring, "how beautiful, oh beautiful," then suddenly he is inside her and it's over.

"Sorry, my dear," he says, and goes to sleep.

They cook spinach and baked halibut. There's a bottle of wine. She has obliged him by wearing one of his shirts, starchy blue-gray, over her skirt. At one point he puts his military hat on her, crowing at the sight like little boy. He's flushed with his conquest and from the whiskey and wine. He tells her jokes and she tries to laugh.

"Next," he announces, chewing cheerfully, his knees against hers under the table, "we're going to do it doggy style. Do you like it like that?"

"No," she says. "Please, not again."

He laughs. "Don't be difficult, my goddess. I'll be more careful of you this time."

After a silence she decides to say, "I've been on the road for four months. It has been very difficult."

"But you had your boyfriend with you," he grins. "How bad can that be?"

"We are just friends," she says so sharply that he puts down his fork and looks at her.

"Right. Tell me another one."

But he is actually, for the first time, looking at her as a person.

"Stavos," she pursues her advantage urgently, "I love my child more than anything in the world. I would die for her. She's in terrible trouble, on the run, I don't know where. I'm in agony. Please don't force me any more. Just let me go."

"My God," he breathes, "what a woman!"

She takes a gulp of wine and dares, "Are you listening to me?"

Meeting her eyes in surprise, he swallows and takes a breath. "I'm listening. I have a sister. Somewhere. She was drafted two years ago, just when she turned seventeen, sent to the western border. We haven't heard from her for many months."

"You must be very worried." Keep him talking.

He tells Crea about his sister, when she was a little girl and how he built her a dollhouse, helped her learn to ride a bike. Sentimental as he gets, his vale of grief is sincere. She listens as if enthralled, and in truth her calculations are muted by admiration for his devotion to his sister, his simplicity of expression, his deep eyes black as night.

He says, "Thank you," when he finishes his story. "Please, will you let me kiss you?"

She offers him her cheek, and he presses his lips there softly.

Upstairs this time, he first lies beside her and strokes her interminably until she responds, and he knows she has.

"You're wet," he says mischievously.

When he lifts her to her hands and knees, she moves with him, moans with him, and she is not, as she had planned, pretending.

In the morning they make love again, in rainy dawn paling the uncurtained window splayed with dripping tree branches. The song of the rain encloses them. Afterwards, looking at his dozing face unlined as a boy's, Crea can't resist lightly kissing him, and decides she must be the most depraved woman in the world.

They have devised a scheme whereby she leaves and he pretends to sleep until his driver returns. But it doesn't work out that way. There's a roar outside, abrupt shouts. Before they can half dress, the room is full of Guards.

◯

Marcel learns about Crea's capture later that day watching television in a computer café. He's sitting with Miro, Linette, and others drinking black coffee. There are no details and the only image shown of her is the old poster. The announcer reports that "Mrs. Hanley is alive and well and safely home," telling Marcel the approach Han will use with her. They all knew Crea, and the mood is somber.

"So," says Marcel, "his story to save his face is that somehow she just wandered off, or maybe was duped. But you can bet she'll be punished."

"He can't keep her against her will forever," Miro argues.

"Yes, he can. Besides, she'll be so crushed by all this, she'll become a zombie again. Jesus, it's all my fault."

Marcel gets up before they can see his tears, hurries out to stand in the doorway facing a wall of rain. Linette follows, lifts her face to him, her bright moon face, and her eyes are terrible.

"You're in love with her. I knew it."

"Linette. I'm sorry. We weren't lovers, I swear it."

"I don't care. Just don't go."

"I can't get near her now, anyway. But yes, I am going. I must try to find her daughter. I have no choice."

Linette's aggrieved hungry eyes, intelligence obliterated by pain, are searching his and finding nothing. With her dimpled paws working each other and her dark primitive stare, she resembles a small animal, a raccoon or a squirrel. Marcel strangles a sob of pity for them both. He knows it's wrong to kiss her but she wants it so much. Her tongue swirling around his is a spiral, a whirlpool, a tornado of lament.

Episode 10

Island

The hurricanes come one right after the other this August. Trees are ripped out by the roots, houses flayed, cornfields smashed. But Tati and Leon's hut, built out of old tires packed with earth, stays solid. It seems they chose wisely locating it down the hill from the main enclave. Out their windows they can see the lake seething surf like ocean, dark to black, no opposite shore but hills jutting straight up on either side.

"It's a good thing we harvested that corn," comments Leon at lunchtime.

He has just returned from helping to fortify a barn, peeling off soaking clothes. Tati keeps her foot pumping at the sewing machine, stitching a shirt. But she glances up long enough to see him clutch a bathrobe around his stooped sinewy form. When he kisses her cheek, she reaches up under the robe to give him a brief caress.

"We'll all be eating corn chowder for weeks," she laughs.

"Corn can be dried," Leon reminds her.

He hangs his clothes by the stove and goes into the bedroom to change. Their two rooms over the two years they've been on the island have accumulated odds and ends of furniture, begged borrowed and built. In refurbishing they had to use what paint was available, resulting in a fire engine red table, a rocking chair half green and half orange, and a multicolored headboard for the bed. Rugs range from hand braided to fake oriental.

Tati warms up chowder, cuts cornbread. Today in this crazed weather she has been thinking too much about Crea in Petit Chapeau still not knowing what has become of Fair. Tati at least knows her child is safe, but what must Crea be suffering, only imagining Fair's fate? There's one computer on the island that works when the solar power can be spared, but no internet access, and in any case eview contact with Canada has been blocked for years. As for letters, getting to the nearest town takes twenty minutes sailing when the wind is good, and then a good hour's walk. Tati has managed to send some, but there's been no response, so her letters probably never even got across the border. She takes solace in Crea's protected situation, much as she dislikes Han. In spite of oppression in Canada, at least there is a strong government that keeps things running. Here in the U.S. the central government has long since disbanded, leaving power vacuums to whoever can seize them. Tati imagines Crea imagining what Fair looks like now, that fireball imp — a woman.

Tully Island in northern Vermont is small and remote, lost in lengthy Lake Willoughby. Its inhabitants hope it's obscure enough not to draw the attention either of roving bandits or swarms of refugees. On maps it's hardly more than a dot, but as the lake continues to wither, more land has been exposed. Now there are almost thirty homes, although some are just a room or two in the old houses, the original mansion and cottages.

"I don't like the sound of that cough," says Tati. "You were so sick last winter."

"Get used to it, sweetie. It doesn't mean anything, it's only bronchial tubes."

She smiles at him sitting on the other side of the stove cradling his bowl, slurping greedily.

"Well, it's certainly not hurting your appetite!"

At seventy, Tati is older by a few years, but Leon seems to have aged more, is more often ill. What's left of his hair is white, his step is slowed, he's a little hard of hearing. He's still sensual and affectionate though, perhaps even more so. In bed when he can't perform the usual way, they manage many interesting alternatives. He's more sensitive to her, too, often willing to talk about and share emotions, which in earlier years he shunned so testily.

At the community meeting that evening they discuss the news that a boat has capsized on Tully's northern coast. The survivors are on the island. There's lively argument over whether to rescue them.

"Where would we put them? We're doubled up as it is now."

"We can't just leave them there to suffer."

"Let them do what we did. We started from scratch."

"The houses and solar panels were already here. There's nothing over there on the north shore except rocks."

"We can't take everybody in, we've already agreed on that!" It's Vinsky again, always ready to take over. Though loose jowled and big bellied, he is wired energy and focus, a swaggering Napoleon. He has a big doughy face in which his very small features are punched like raisins. He pushes, "Look at the minutes of the last meeting. We're not allowing any more people to settle on the island, remember? Do we have to have this conversation again, folks?"

Tati looks around at the faces she knows so well, worn and anxious, grim. The room, once the spacious parlor of the summer mansion, is lined with makeshift chairs and keeps only faded maroon and gold wallpaper as a reminder of its former splendor. It's true, they can't grow food for many more people, the warming lake is greening from algae choking off oxygen that fish need, and getting supplies in town is chancy. To buy things you must have money, or at least good barter, and even then you may well not find what you want. They have to think of themselves, if only for the sake of the children. There are twelve children now, three of them born on the island. But Tati knows that if they don't help those strangers, something more of their own humanity will be lost, already frayed as it is.

"Let's bring them in," she says. They turn to her, listening. She's one of the elders. "We can give them another boat. They probably won't want to stay here anyway."

"We can explain the situation."

"Right. They'll understand. At least we won't let them starve to death."

The next day when the wind has quieted, a group that includes their only doctor sets out. Old Dr. Dom plodding resolutely, toting a medical bag so shabby its black has turned gray. A tattered looking parade, one of them with a rifle, a horse with blankets and stretchers strapped to its back. Unspoken on all their minds is the leaden question: what if this keeps happening? What if the invaders resist leaving? Will we soon have to fight and kill to keep our homes?

The search party returns by a rose evening light made brilliant by lake reflections. There is no wind at all and the soaked earth-smelling air is heavy. The lake laps the shore so languidly there's no sound. Tomorrow it will be hot again. All the boat's passengers have survived, three of them, with a dog. Only one is on a stretcher, a sunken-eyed woman wrapped in blankets. A boy and a young woman are riding the horse.

The whole community gathers to receive them. Curiosity, resentment, foreboding. Not even a grown man to add muscle, just three more mouths to feed.

As soon as the young woman jumps off the horse, she cries, "Is my grandmother here? Tatyana?"

Tati slumps against Leon. Electric shock. It's Fair.

○

Han makes sure that Crea knows Stavos was executed. By firing squad, with before and after pictures she has to look at. First he's standing blindfolded and then he's crumpled on the ground in a mass of blood. And she has to say she's glad, because the official story is that she was the victim of two unscrupulous men. First she was kidnapped by Marcel, and when she escaped and tried to return home to her husband, Stavos captured her and took vile advantage. Her reward for buying into this tale has been restoration to full status as the general's devoted wife. Han likes the story, not only because it saves him face, but because it portrays her as helpless without his protection.

But Crea now knows she's not helpless, does not have to be a victim. Her months on the run gave her a dawning awareness of her own strength, and the months she's been home have shown her the power she can wield by deception. She gratifies Han with her contrite acquiescence, while keeping her true self at a scornful distance.

But this separation of realities is taking its toll. She has no confidante, trusts no one, and her urgent discussions with herself are wearing thin. By now she has figured out that what she ran away from in Montreal was not sex, but love: she's in love with Marcel, and has been for years. And of course she had to flee love — not only would it have tied her down just when she'd discovered a real lead to Fair, but most of all it would have absorbed her just when she was finding out who she was, falling in love with herself. The experience with Stavos was like a perverse little microcosm of her transition: the coercion she'd come to expect leading to the radiance of sex between equals that she hadn't felt in years. The dawn of forgiving herself. She still harbors a vague affection for the lieutenant's childish egotism, his tragic hubris, his young body, and she mourns his blood. In Petit Chapeau she often feels she is not here, in this room, in this bed, at this table, but floating far above, gazing down. It's dizzying, and more and more confusing. There are cuts in her palm where she has dug in her nails to make herself concentrate on the actual situation.

She asks permission to visit Fleur's grave. Permission has been denied before, but she doesn't ask for much, and this time Han agrees. So one morning she stands in the boiling August air, a hot wind blowing dust, in front of the little gray headstone that states, "Fleur Chamois, 1968-2048, joyeuse avec son Dieu." Underneath, a pile of ashes. But all around in the fiery sun and sky, Fleur's free spirit, Fleur's subversive soul.

"Congratulations," sighs Fleur. "You did it. I knew you could."

"But I'm back here," murmurs Crea. "I failed." She glances over at the chauffeur standing by the limousine. No, he can't hear. "Will this go on forever? I can't stand it."

Fleur says, "You'll find a way. Don't worry. Keep your eyes open."

"For what? No one would dare to help me."

Crea goes down on her knees, palms swimming the dusty ground, supplicating. The wind wraps soil over her hands, strands hair from under her hat across her mouth.

"Don't worry. I will help you again," promises Fleur.

So visits to Fleur become a weekly occurrence, the only time Crea feels restored to wholeness. There, she's anchored, sees clearly. Han is still supplied daily with a report of exactly what she's been doing, but the graveyard visits are now as routine on those reports as appointments with her hair stylist or consultations with her cook. Besides, he no longer reads them obsessively.

One day as she kneels there with Fleur, she hears a shot. She starts up to see the chauffeur get out his gun and run off after something. In the same moment arms come around her, holding fast.

A voice she knows. "Crea!"

She looks up at a grimy bearded face under a low black hat, into the eyes of Marcel. He draws her into a clump of bushes where they crouch and he says, "I have news of Fair and we have only minutes. She's in Vermont with your mother on an island called Tully in Lake Willoughby. She's well."

"How can I…will you..?"

"I can't do anything now. We've been spotted and we're on the run. Try to find a boat."

"A boat…?"

But Marcel is pulling away, watching the chauffeur in the distance. She has the courage to say, "I love you," and to bring him to a swift deep kiss. Then he's gone and she sees the chauffeur running around hysterically looking for her.

She creeps fearfully out, explaining unnecessarily, "I was hiding, I was frightened."

"Everything's fine, Mrs. Hanley. Just some troublemakers. I scared them away."

That evening, presiding with Han over after-dinner drinks in the library, Crea is fighting giddy joy. She has to work hard to keep on her face the calm gracious mask, a little appropriate sadness thrown in, that so charms everyone. Only Ruella Leonard looks at her too keenly. This is a woman who knows female machinations, thinks Crea, she will be hard to fool. Ruella in fact has been one of Han's sexual flings, unsuspected by her usually astute husband. Crea stares her down, taking an acid satisfaction in knowing that since she has returned home in her renewed beauty, Han has been too busy mounting his wife to have a lot of energy left for others.

The glass doors to the garden are closed against the pressing heat, the whole house air conditioned. As usual the General has a solid supply of electricity, supplemented by solar and wind power collected from miles around. This summer there have been over five hundred deaths in the town due to heat stroke alone. Most people don't even remember what air conditioning is.

Marguerite, bustling in sleeveless black, wafts a tray of bloom-shaped glasses of Courvoisier among the guests. The mood is desultory, smug. Border incidents have been down, and the Credos are rumored to be scattering.

"So, dear," croons Ruella, "any news of your daughter?"

She lolls in purple silk, red nailed brown hand cupping her drink, feet in lavender silk shoes tucked daintily together. The question is in incredibly bad taste, but that never stopped Ruella. Instantly Crea looks over at Han, to hide the lightness that must be in her eyes at mention of Fair. He's holding forth by the mantelpiece regaling Lieutenant and Mrs. Renaud.

"Han has had a good report," she says carefully, "just recently. Fair is said to be up north somewhere in the Manicougan region." She wonders bitterly if he knows she's actually in Vermont. Surely he knows she's left Canada. She dares to meet Ruella's eyes for a second, then bends them to her lap. "We are hopeful."

"Why hasn't she come home?"

"Well, we don't know what the circumstances are, do we? I mean, she could be held against her will. But at least, we know she's alive."

"I'm sure the general will find her."

"Oh, yes. It's just a matter of time."

Throughout this bland exchange, the two women have been dueling with eyes and body language. Ruella has shifted to lean forward.

"So glad you're back home, poor dear," she lows in a parting shot. "That must have been a terrible ordeal for you."

Crea knows that if there's one thing Ruella is sure of, it's that Crea left Han of her own free will. She allows herself to smile broadly at this parry, even tilts her head confidentially, and whispers, "Han is so happy."

Ruella's black eyes snap in annoyance.

That night as Han grunts and pants over Crea, slapping her and cursing her for a whore and slut as he loves to do, and she is whimpering obligingly, Marcel's kiss is in her mouth and her mind floats in a magical boat on wide waters, sailing swiftly to Fair.

◯

"Priests," says Tati.

She hands the binoculars to Fair. They're standing on a high rock squinting out at a triple-decker yacht heading undeniably for their dock. The sound of the motor is strange, grating alien, throbbing all the air.

"You're right. White robes. Must be."

A crowd is gathering on the shore below. Wagons of newly gathered hay rest idle, a herd of sheep mills distractedly about, bins of squash and onions sit untended, on the decks of fishing boats nets lie dropped. Catching the anxiety in the air, children stop screaming excitedly at the novelty and creep closer to their parents.

"They won't hurt us," Tati says tersely.

"But then what do they want?"

"To convert everyone, of course. Leon and I have had dealings with Zorians before, in the camp."

On the road Fair has run into Zorians, too, arrogant swaggering youths taunting girls with the specter of hell if they don't convert by having sex with them. She had ignored them, climbing into the wagon with Iris,

Miles braving it out. But she doesn't know about priests. They must have some kind of official power. They must have ways.

Fair steals frequent glances at her grandmother, eased each time. She's been on the island almost a month now, but she still can't stop looking at Tati, this beloved old woman who is like coming home. Fair was nine last time she saw her, in that almost mythical time back in Massachusetts when she was leaving with her parents for the chimera of Canada. Tati strides tall and purposeful still, like a flamingo, skinny legs, wide girth, untamed abundant gray hair, gaunt face. A face beautiful in its wrinkle webs with a smile like dawn.

Autumn fog has lifted off the lake, letting in sunlight that will soon be blazing but for now feels soft and benign. Remaining clumps of mist waft against the hulks of steep hills. Smells of clover and pine mingle with fresh cut hay and apples. The whole scene could be such a peaceful sight — by the shining lake the oddly assorted houses, old-fashioned cottages interspersed with new abodes crafted from stones or tires and topped with glinting solar panels. Higher up the grand old mansion dotted with shutters painted in different colors. Farther back the battered red barn, yellow fields, dazzling blue waves of chicory flowers, swirling wind turbine, clumps of pines. Fair in a shudder puts her arm around her grandmother and says, "Don't worry." Tati squeezes her in return, tosses back in a tone lightly ironic, "Of course, men of God. No problem."

In fact, the priests are quite genteel. There are five of them, in their 20s and 30s except for their leader, a grizzled dwarfish humpback named Brother Cobb. He addresses the crowd in a kindly manner.

"My beloveds, thank you in Jesus' name for your welcome. When Zoria gives birth to our Lord, and he returns to walk amongst us once again, may he find you in good standing and save you from eternal fire. You are all good people at heart, I am sure, and you want to confess your sins and submit your souls to the Mother of Christ. We're here to give you that opportunity. Thank you."

He asks for permission to set up an altar on a ledge in front of the old mansion: the hallmark inverted cross, a couple of torches, and the coffin shaped container all too familiar to Tati.

"That box is where we put our valuables when we convert," Tati wryly explains to Fair.

"We don't have any valuables."

"They'll think of something."

For lunch a long row of tables is set up under the trees for the kind of banquet usually held for celebrations. As Fair hustles back and forth helping to set places, she's sure this is not a good idea. Without time for a community meeting and no united front, into the gap have stepped busybodies like Stella and Vinsky. Stella loves to show off her cooking skills and is enthusiastic about authority of any kind; Vinsky just gets his kicks from giving orders. But the festive air is dampened by the conspicuous absence of half the island's inhabitants.

"Here," Vinsky barks at Fair, "Put a pitcher of water on each table."

"We'll have to purify a whole new barrel," Fair objects.

His look says, "You twit, you don't belong here anyway," as his lips pretend to smile. His hairy hand splays at her. "Do what you can. The priests deserve respect."

Her eyebrows reply, "No, they don't!" But she doesn't argue.

One of Fair's jobs is dining room duty at the main house, where anyone can sign up to share meals. Tati and Leon often prefer to eat alone at home, but Fair likes to join the others, especially Kiva, also seventeen. The girls make a polarized pair, one sprightly small with red hair, the other languorous lanky, olive skinned. This afternoon, Raven trotting close, they take their plates of food up to the porch of the main house where a breeze cools. From here they can watch the proceedings at the banquet as well as the broad expanse of water, rocks, and pines. Up high an owl hunches. The smog is light today, and they can see layers of steep hills marching down the lake. Waves tongue the shore indifferently.

"There goes our winter supply of corn," notes Kiva. "Stella made fritters for the creeps."

"Right, and the corn was already down because of the storms."

"We ran out of food the first year. I was fourteen. I remember, for months we were never not hungry. Thank God for potatoes."

"Kiva, when you came, were you the first ones?"

"My family and me, two brothers and my father I mean, and six others. There already were some people, here in the big house. But they were living like crazies. They didn't know how to grow things and they didn't dare leave the island. Wow they were glad to see us. But it was hard. My oldest brother out fishing was killed in a storm, and my father almost died of diarrhea before we learned how to purify the water."

"My father died from cholera," confides Fair. Then to stop Kiva's response, "Look at that ridiculous ass-kissing going on down there. The best tablecloth no less. I don't know why they're treating them like royalty. They're conmen."

Kiva puts her hand on Fair's shoulder. "My mother too. Cholera."

Fair remembers tears but her eyes are dry. Raven's head has appeared just beneath her hand, and she strokes his ears, lingers with his warm silky comfort. She has come to trust Kiva enough to tell her about Seth. She has sent a letter to the town he used to live in, where perhaps his family still is, though sending a letter across the border, or anything anywhere these days, is little more than an act of faith. But there's this prancing little glint of hope lighting her way: if he ever gets the letter, he will know where she is, and he will come.

Fair briefly as breath tilts her head to brush Kiva's, presses her hand to the hand on her shoulder. For awhile they keep silence. Then Fair pulls out her harmonica and starts a tune she and Seth used to play. The sharp quavering notes of the harmonica pierce the sodden air.

○

Crea is seasick again. Lying on coils of rope below in the bow, she has not dared to try for fresh air. Boats leaving Canada are generally not of interest to the Guards, but this cargo would be: Han must have sounded the alarm by now. Everyone will be looking for her, and if she's caught, this time he will certainly not be lenient. But Lake Mephremagog flows freely from one country to the other, the border but a ripple here in the wide waters. And only one person on board knows she's there, or rather only one officially. Crea suspects the whole crew has an inkling that the bow holds a stowaway. They're being paid too well not to know it, and too well to say so.

She drinks a little water carefully, nibbles on a biscuit. She's got to keep up her strength. The fishing boat pitches like a captured wild thing, the October storm pelting monsoons. The permanent wet is cold, clammy through to her skin. Crea is miserable in every bone, but she's exultant. She's on her way.

○

Seth and Marcel stagger out of the storm into the barn. It's dry and dark, smells of stale hay and manure. Three tawny cows and a pony regard them with vague curiosity. The cows chew and drool, the pony snorts. The men peel off their soaking clothes, wring them out, hang them on stalls, rifle their backpacks for something dry to wear, but nothing is. Seth quickly nestles into hay, Marcel takes a moment to press himself against a cow for warmth, then dives into the hay. They share a soggy loaf of bread and flask of rum as they talk, barely able to see each other's faces. They have a flashlight but dare not use it.

"The coast is only about ten miles away now," says Marcel. "The incinerator we aim to close down will be on low operation tomorrow, Sunday, so our timing is right."

"So far so good. Should we hitchhike again?"

"Don't think so. We were damn lucky with that guy with the wagon today, but that was risky."

"He still could squeal," Seth says.

"Why should he?"

"Who knows. Money?"

Marcel is annoyed with Seth's cynicism. The kid is barely twenty-one, more than twenty years younger. He's supposed to be innocent and gullible. Instead, Seth is the tough guy of the two, the swaggerer, the skeptic. They met at a Credo meeting in Montreal shortly after Crea left. They sized each other up warily, the younger one with the insecure bravado of his liberation from slavery, the older man with no patience for a headstrong novice. Respect came reluctantly, in spite of themselves. Then one day they discovered their connection, and embraced like brothers.

"Fair? Fair Franklin's mother?" Seth yelled.

"Fair's mother, yes, Crea, my friend Crea. You were held with Fair at Baron Lemoyne's?"

"Fair is my, is my…she's the one. I have a letter from her, my uncle brought it to me."

"You know where she is?" Marcel jumped from his chair, collared Seth wildly. "Where? Tell me where Fair is!"

Seth stood up and pointedly removed Marcel's hand before replying. "Lake Willoughby."

As soon as Marcel got the details, he began planning to somehow get in touch with Crea, risking his life and even Miro's operations, but single minded until it was done. Staking out that damn graveyard for days, his companions doubting his sanity. Worth it for that one cosmic kiss.

Now, in the dim warm barn, belly temporarily happy, Marcel succumbs to his gratitude and affection, and answers quietly, "Well, this is our last assignment, so let's hope."

"Then," sighs Seth, "we can go find them. Our women."

"We've done twelve missions now. Disabled two incinerators, drained three oil barrels, freed six prisoners…"

"We made too many promises to Miro. Especially this last one. He doesn't need us for this one. There's a huge cadre of Credos here in Nova Scotia."

"They don't have our experience."

"Yeah, so we're heroes."

"We'll be out of here tomorrow night."

"Fair, here I come. Here comes your man."

○

Tati and Leon don't want Fair to go to the Zorian rally this evening. Fair tries to be gentle in her resistance, but it's not the first time they've been overprotective. Don't they remember what she's been through, for

God's sake? She's not some little lamb fresh out of high school, which they probably were at her age.

It hasn't been easy, all three of them living together. In the euphoria of the first days after her arrival, they outfitted their little pantry area with a narrow bed and Fair was more than happy to sleep snugly amongst canned fruits, dried vegetables, and potato piles. But it's dampish and windowless in there. She has begun scheming with Kiva, who lives with her father and brother, to build themselves a little shelter of their own, at least for the warmer season. But the hurdles of time and materials are daunting. When Fair isn't helping with meals, she's trying to catch up on her education. When Kiva isn't climbing scaffolding helping to build the island's second wind turbine, she's learning to card wool. As for materials, they'll have to be ingenious as well as persuasive to come up with what they need.

"I'm just curious about the priests," argues Fair, "I want to hear what they have to say."

"You know what they have to say," counters Tati. "They've said it, over and over."

"Well, it doesn't sound so dire, Gran, really it doesn't. Sort of pitiful, when you think about it."

"It's pitiful all right," intones Leon.

"Nobody should go, it just encourages them," says Tati, beating her brain to think of the right phrase to convince the child. She doesn't want her precious charge to get anywhere near the conniving, corrupt Zorians. "Anyway, it will depress you to see how some people make spectacles of themselves."

They're all sitting at the red table after breakfast, sipping the last of their chicory coffee. It's going to be another hot day. Already a shimmer of heat trembles over the lake. Leon is shirtless under his overalls, Tati in a gauzy sundress, Fair in shorts and a multicolored top with string straps. She crafted the outfit herself out of someone's old pants, ribbons, two panels of cloth. Its brevity suits her wiry slim form, her darting twirling movements like a little eel. Her fiery hair is longer now, wisping at her neck.

"Don't tell me you're afraid I'll decide to convert," Fair laughs.

"Well," snorts Leon, "I know you wouldn't be that stupid."

"Those men are very charismatic," counters Tati. "You're young, you never know…"

"That's it, Gran," Fair cries, standing quickly and draining her mug. "I've got to go to work. If you don't think I have a brain, I can't convince you."

"Oh dear," sighs Tati. "Now I've insulted you. I give up."

She and Leon watch the girl through the window as she climbs swift as a gazelle up the hill. Past a clutch of grazing sheep and rows of apple trees, some uprooted by storms, their gaping wounds of root tendrils dripping black soil. She looks like a flower, thinks Tati, a fairy goddess, a Botticelli painting, a vortex of the life force. If only her mother could see her now, if only her mother were here.

"Don't say a word," orders Leon, standing behind Tati massaging her neck and shoulders. "None of your doom and gloom. She'll be fine. She's a lot like you, you know."

Tati closes her eyes, turns into Leon's embrace. She knows this time of hope is only a reprieve, not a rescue.

Episode 11

Last Thursday in November

Tati wakes up vaguely, her cheek on Leon's thigh. It's not dark yet, she can make out the time on the bedside table clock: 7:40. Outside the round window tacked with fishnet, pines and oaks gyrate in a brisk breeze in purple autumn light. Screams from her nightmare echo still, but she dismisses them, snuggles back down with a kiss and a smile on Leon's sticky groin. His face is obscured by her leg across his chest, but he gives a sleepy grunt, and reaches down to lightly stroke her hair. They must have dozed for maybe half an hour, clambering in here playfully not long after dinner. The little room is hot but the wind filters across their damp limbs caressing.

Suddenly Tati starts up rigid. Jolted, Leon wails, "Hey."

He's on one elbow frowning at her standing naked at attention like someone shot in frozen shock just before falling.

She says, "The screaming hasn't stopped."

◯

When Fair had arrived at the rally, Kiva persuaded her to sit with the other "virgins" in special seats reserved for them.

Fair laughed. "Neither one of us is a virgin."

"Theoretically, we are, we're the right age."

"The age the priests have the hots for, you mean."

"Whatever. Who cares?"

"You are lacking in piety, my dear," smirked Fair. "Don't you want to be saved?"

"Hey, I'll convert if I can have that one over there."

Giggling and pointing out favorable features in the Zorians, they took their places among the other young women in the front row. The stage set up on the jutting ledge above was lit with torches at either end, waved a dozen red and gold flags with the inverted cross. In their white robes the priests sat in a row on chairs draped with white. To the left Fair could see strands of streaming crimson clouds in the sky darkening over the trees, to the right the orchard weighted red with fruit. Behind her sat expectantly about half of Tully's population, including some of the children, and beyond them the dock, the rocking boats, the greenish lake churning whitecaps.

Drums beat slowly sonorous. Gusting wind billowed out the flags and all the white cloth, sails of glory concurring in the urgency of Brother Cobb's exhortations.

"Beloveds!" he shouted. "We are gathered here to fall down in abject
worship to the divine Zoria, the new mother of Christ our Redeemer. She
carries him proudly and tenderly in her womb, until the day comes when
he is born again." His voice lowered gently as he spoke to their hearts.
"Believe me, I know how hard it's been for you. God did not want to do
this, to visit this desperation upon you. But it was the only way to bring
you back to him."

The sadness in his voice tapped all Fair's grief. Kiva began wiping tears,
and sobs were breaking out around them.

"Yes, it's been hard," crooned Brother Cobb. "So much pain, so much
fear, so much despair. Oh, my Beloveds! Earth that used to be so good to
us brought to this doom and destruction!"

Fair's cynicism met with a seductive delusion. She knew Zoria was
a lie through and through, but the very glimmer of mercy for the world
entranced her for a mesmerizing moment. Trumpets blared and all the
priests rose, their arms spread upward, faces to heaven. They began to
chant, supplicating, pale robes writhing in the wild wind. Just as the sky
blackened, the first priest fell.

At first everyone thought this was part of the act. In their vulnerable
state they could half believe that Brother Cobb had summoned the storm,
that the priest was felled by a trance of devotion. But in another second,
when Brother Cobb ran over to help him and sprang back, the truth
dawned like fireworks. People started running, screaming. "Fever! The
fever! Ebola!"

Kiva's brother fought through the crowd to grab her and force her
away, yelling, "Dad says get to the boat! Get in the boat!"

Now Tati and Leon have pulled on clothes haphazardly and are
rushing outside. Fair has dashed halfway home and stops to look back,
clutching a tree against the gale. Rain is slashing, blinding. She's soaked,
battered by the wind, crouching to the ground, numbly watching the
hysteria, people sloshing around aimlessly in muddy torrents. She hears
Raven barking, Tati and Leon calling her, and she turns and stumbles toward their voices.

○

Crea pours her pearls into the man's outstretched palm. This house
is making her nervous. She's been here for three days now, on the north
shore of Lake Willoughby, waiting for another boat. Three days is way
too long to be in one place. Han could be enraged enough to pursue her
across the border and she's lost the advantage of her sudden head start.
Her only attempt at disguise is hair pulled down flat around her face, and
baggy shorts she bought from a fisherman. Her filmy sleeveless blouse is

too fine — soiled and wrinkled, it's still clearly silk. People stare at her leather sandals.

The man's stubby fingers come down over the pearls in a fist. Her room is unbreathably stuffy, darkened by dark curtains against the last rays of sun. He steps away towards the door, still with the same knowing, sarcastic look on his face.

He repeats, "Five in the morning, sharp. Be on the dock."

"Five."

"Wind coming up. Rain tonight. Should be all right tomorrow."

"Thanks again."

She lifts the curtain to watch him saunter away. That was the last of her jewelry. Canadian money is worth nothing here. As she has a hundred times, she stares down the lake in the direction of Tully Island, conjuring it up out of her heart. On either side jut the precipices of tall dark hills. The gray-green water bubbles at the sand. The sky to the east is darkening, but to the west wispy lavender clouds decking the declining sun still scud brightly. The wind is heavy with smells of pine and fish. She tries to guess which of the boats belongs to tomorrow's captain. He said it was small, did he say twenty feet? She hopes it's that little blue one, it looks so jaunty and determined.

Suddenly she sees her sailor racing back toward the dock and at the same moment the whole sky turns black and rain jabs her face. The boats are slamming into each other. More people race out to lash the boats steady, or try to pull the small ones to land. But nothing much is getting accomplished except a lot of shouting, because the hurricane is grabbing things like toys and throwing them around. Crea fights the window shut just as someone pounds on the door yelling, "Get down to the cellar! Hurry up!"

It's black as night and she inches her way down the stairs. In the cellar there are lamps and it's dry. Crea stands against a wall clutching her travel bag and a blanket. From outside come sounds of thudding, smashing, cracking. A few people are crying, but others are having little conversations, settling in. She soon realizes she needs to stake out a space, so many people are crowding past her. She sets up a kind of nest under the stairs next to a moist-eyed woman and her small son. Someone starts simmering soup on a portable stove. The landlady announces there'll be food for everyone. Cooking smells, at least for now, overcome the reek of damp clothes and sweat.

A few hours later many people are asleep, and all but one of the lamps are out, when two newcomers arrive. The men stand on the last step easing off their dripping shirts, looking for a place to sit. One sweeps a flashlight around, prompting hisses and complaints. Others press them for news. "Is it still crazy out there?" "Is anybody hurt?" "Are the houses ok?"

Crea asks, "Did you happen to notice the boats?"

The flashlight swings around to shine in her face as the man holding it shouts, "Crea!" Blinded, she can't see him at first, but she knows who it is. Marcel is in her arms before she can say a word. He's drenched, he smells awful, his beard is matted, but she holds onto him for dear life, sobbing and laughing, kisses him for a long time, feeds at his hot mouth. When they come up for air, people are staring at them, some smiling.

Marcel's companion, a stocky black-haired youth, is glowing happily. "You must be Fair's mother."

All three sit in a close circle with crossed legs, urgently exchanging stories. When Crea finds out that Seth was held with Fair in captivity, she takes his hand in hers and won't let go, a lifeline to her child. She wants every detail of the ordeal. Seth gladly obliges but his eyes are glazing over with fatigue. Soon he's crouched down in a fetal position, fast asleep. Crea and Marcel curl together and continue talking, interspersed with kisses. Only when they wake up do they realize they've been sleeping too.

Late the next morning, when the announcement comes that it's safe to go out, they climb the stairs to her room. How wonderful it will be to get in bed, thinks Crea, to lie down in bed with Marcel. At last. But when she opens her door, there's sky above. A huge plank has crashed through the roof, the floor is streaming with water, and the bed is soaked.

They groan in disappointment and despair, holding each other. Crea's desire is so strong it almost sickens her. She pulls open her blouse, grinds her breasts against his bare chest. He cups them to his face, open mouthed. They strip off each other's clothes, she climbs him, he lifts her onto him. His arms tight under her, she pulls him in, he's pulsing to her womb, they ride in all their terrible hunger, beating together as if resuscitating the whole earth, singing their moans of love. Then for a moment he slows, says, "Look at me."

She pulls back to meet his entranced eyes, and cries out softly.

○

Vinsky takes over Tully. Even before the storm ends, he orders the priests quarantined, designates a site behind the main house, decrees caretakers and guards. Anybody with the first signs of fever must be taken there immediately, by force if necessary. His aides march around shouting through bullhorns. Nobody objects. His cool head and single-minded focus are an anchor in the chaos.

During that week people start keeling over like the uprooted trees that are strewn everywhere. One day Tati is standing in her doorway when Miles comes by, wearing the blue armband that signifies he's a Vinsky aide.

His gloves and the face mask hanging around his neck are homemade with mismatched patterns.

"Hey, Tati," Miles says wearily. "Just checking to see how you all are."

Instead of greeting him with motherly affection as usual, Tati replies coldly, "I see you're an authority now."

He blinks in hurt. "Got drafted you might say," he apologizes, "but anything I can do to help."

"You can go away."

Now Miles sees the look on her face, sees that she's blocking the door.

"Where's Leon?" he asks carefully, his fear almost matching her own.

"Not here."

"He is here, isn't he?"

Tati hates with a killing rage this pious pushy boy she loved only yesterday. She can tell that he sees the tears spilling out from her glaring eyes.

"He's sick isn't he?" Miles insists gently.

She starts beating at him with her fists but weakly, and he sorrowfully deflects them, holds her in an embrace, puts her in a chair. He goes briefly into the bedroom.

He comes out, gives Tati a cup of water, pats her shoulder, stands awkwardly in his clownish mask, eyes gleaming. He says, "You know what we have to do."

After the boy has gone, it seems only minutes before urgent people are invading her home and carrying off her heart's blood on a stretcher. They won't even let her kiss him, they hold her back.

All the while Leon is dying, Tati is not allowed to touch him. In some ways that's the hardest part. The quarantined area is fenced in, the sick lying on blankets in rows on the ground. Overhead they are protected scantily by pieces of tarp spread between tree branches. Everyone knows that if there's another heavy rain, the tent will collapse. But what can they do? As soon as anyone shows a sign of the fever they are hustled into isolation here, tended only by a chosen few. Tati is not allowed to volunteer; this service is limited to the young and strong. Out of the thirty-two who have fallen ill, fifteen have died by the end of the second week, including all the priests. Because they went first, the priests got a row of Zorian crosses, but lately the dead are just buried two or three together in trenches.

Anyway, it's not likely to rain again soon. Since the outbreak there's been only stifling heat, probably another drought coming. Tati stands by the fence where she can see Leon. She watches him toss and turn, bleed and vomit. Her heart and arms ache to hold and tend him. They haven't even had a chance to say goodbye.

"Gran, please come home," pleads Fair. "You need to rest."

"Let me be. Go away. You shouldn't be here."

"I brought you some cheese and a fresh cucumber. Here, drink this raspberry juice. I chilled it in the lake."

"Child," intones Tati. "Stop it. There's nothing you can do for me. You don't understand. I don't want to live. I want to die too."

Fair gazes helplessly at her grandmother's beloved profile, haggard. She wants to hold her but doesn't try.

"When my father died," Fair says instead, "I felt dead for a while."

Around them and around the groaning sick the gilded autumn leaves lie absolutely still in the weighted air. Sparrows are taking a dust bath nearby, flailing up the soil with their wings, chirping and arguing. Their chatter mingles with the moans of misery and pain in perverse contretemps. The women watch while a young man — even though his nose and mouth are covered and he's wearing bulky protective clothing, Fair knows it's Kiva's brother — tries to get Leon to drink something. It doesn't work, Leon gurgles it back up.

Fair turns away her eyes but Tati does not.

"I thought we'd make it," Tati whispers. "I thought we'd survive again. I think it's the same ebola strain that hit the camp we were in. Oh, why did he get it and not me?"

"Blood, sweat — bodily fluids they say, but who knows? One of the priests could've handed him something. Or someone who had close contact with a priest."

"The priests brought death with them."

"Look, Gran, the days are getting shorter. It will be dark soon. Come on."

Finally Tati, staggering with fatigue, allows herself to be led away. Fair is muscular but smaller, and her grandmother's weight is almost more than she can manage. They progress slowly, back past the main house, whose whole right wing was smashed in. It's being repaired quite quickly, even though the fishing boats take priority. On the path down to their house they pass the ugly funereal procession of the fallen apple trees, every one of them uprooted. Great quantities of applesauce and cider are resulting from them, but Tully has no orchard now.

Tati stands still by her door. "I can't bear to go in. He's not there."

"No, gran, he's not there. And you have to go in. Be brave. Be brave for Leon."

Tati falls into bed and asleep. Fair eats the cucumber with bread and smoked fish, sitting outside watching the motionless lake, still browned from mudslides, hazing in sunset. These days she's also been consoling Kiva, whose father drowned when they capsized trying to escape the fever in the storm, and Miles whose mother Iris died in the first week. Suffering is as constant as the stultifying heat. There hasn't been one moment when either she or her spirit could take a real breath.

Fair remembers when she was twelve, living contentedly with her mother and Han in that gorgeous house, with servants and horses and all the music lessons she could handle. Grief over her father's death was tucked safely away, she had a best friend and a crush on a boy named Owen. It wasn't much more than five years ago. But her mind curls around the memory like a dream, suckling it for nourishment, for the incredible assurance that life has not always been brutal. That time seems as fantastic as a fairy tale.

"Sweetpea," Crea used to plead, trying to persuade Fair to wear a sweater or finish homework or eat her vegetables, "sweetpea, make your mama happy." Her mother's face, its love and concern, its slightly bemused pride, rarely ordering but bargaining with Fair. Her mother's glowing golden-haloed face smiling.

Fair's eyes are dry but she opens her mouth in a soundless howl.

Tati, tossing, fears even in her sleep that Leon will die when she's not there, they will take him away. And that's what happens. When she wakes up with the first light and is hurrying to get ready to return to the quarantine area, someone comes by to inform her that he's gone, already buried. Tati goes back into the bedroom, lies down, does not speak a word or move.

Fair cleans up the kitchen, sweeps, plans meals, washes, gets dressed, knowing the doctor will not have a minute for a woman only mourning the love of her life. So on her way to the main house she stops by the shack where Miles lives.

"Fair, hi." His grin is a shadow of itself, but he high fives her enthusiastically. "How you doing?"

She gives him a hug and they talk about Iris.

"Leon is gone too," she tells him. "But look, Miles, I'm worried about Gran. She hasn't eaten much for days and now she won't even move. Can I see your mother's herbal book? You used to tell me about some of the people she cured when she was a healer back home. A reddish book, kind of beat up, colorful cover?

"Sure." He steers Fair around clutter to hand her the book. "Keep it."

"Oh, no, your mother's precious book..."

"I mean it. You're the one who should have it. You're a healer at heart, Fair." He takes a small brown bottle from a shelf. "Here, try this for your Gran. You put it in some alcohol I think. Put it in wine for her."

"What is it?"

"It's from flowers. Calming, my mom used to say."

She looks at him, now taller than she is, his freckled boy's face weighted and set beyond his years. What he's been through. What he did for her and

Raven. How he took care of his mother. How brave he's being with what he must be feeling.

"Miles," she says, "you are the best."

○

"Ready to come about," warns Marcel.

Crea and Seth duck the swinging mast. She clambers up to sit cross-legged on the bow, peering into the distance at Tully's shore. The late afternoon heat shimmers a glinting curtain blurring her view.

"There it is," she cries. "I can see the dock, I can see people!"

"The dock looks shot, though, must've been badly hit," notes Marcel. "Damn, the wind just died again."

Seth clambers around tightening the sails, cursing the fickle wind. Crea reports every detail of what she sees, and imagines she sees. It took weeks after the storm to come up with a boat, and they were forced to settle for a pitiful wreck they had to repair. Innumerable times on the way down the lake they have all had to stop what they were doing and bail water like crazy.

It's Seth who sees the black flag first. "What the hell?"

Crea is frightened by his tone. "What, what? Oh God, Marcel, Marcel, what does a black flag mean?"

Seth says, "Sickness. I think it means, you know, cholera or ebola or something."

Crea feels her hot skin ice over. In silence they watch the inch by inch approach of Tully Island. Suddenly a canoe darts out from the dock, headed for them. It moves quickly but the time it takes to get there is excruciating for the newcomers. Basically becalmed, sails drooping, they watch the scene — people gathering on the shore among chunks of broken boats and fallen trees, behind them the collection of odd looking shelters, above it all the handsome mansion a token of faraway times. There are three men in the canoe.

"They paddle like Natives," mutters Seth in admiration.

When it gets close enough, one of them yells, "This is Tully Island. What d'you want?"

Marcel stands up. "To come ashore," he replies, keeping his tone neutral.

"Nope. Not possible, I'm afraid. We've got ebola here."

Crea cries out. "Please! My daughter! Fair, you know Fair?"

The name has an immediate effect on the men, whose shoulders slump from military stance to huddled conference, gesturing and nodding. Meanwhile, Crea shouts more questions and pleas. "Is my mother here too? Tati? Are they okay?"

Finally one of the men says, "We can ask our captain, Judge Vinsky."

"The fever has pretty much burned itself out," confides another. "We keep the flag up to discourage people."

"Wait here. Wait til we talk to the judge. We'll be back."

The canoe takes off.

From the porch of the big house where she's helping to prepare dinner, Fair watches with other staff the approach of the strange sailboat and its encounter with the canoe. After the canoe returns, its news reaches her by an ocean of voices rippling up person to person from the shore. When she hears it, she says to somebody, "Run, tell my Gran," and races for the shore.

Vinsky is holding forth. "Consider, my friends," he says to the crowd. "Do we really need more people on this island? Think about it."

Fair takes off her shoes and slips behind him into the water, paddles beside a floating log to stay out of sight. Some people can see her but they don't say a word. She knows that Vinsky will probably be persuaded to come around, but not until he has flexed his power muscles. The water is warm. She's a very good swimmer but she's afraid her wildly beating blood will make her faint.

Marcel holds Crea while she calms. "We're going ashore," he promises.

"Damn right," growls Seth.

Crea goes back up to sit on the prow, the closest she can get to the island, peering at it so hard her eyes hurt. Seth and Marcel confer quietly about their options. Fair keeps her grip on the log until her head clears, then she strikes out at full speed. Crea spots the approaching log, sees the reddish head depart from it, the strokes of girlish arms. She knows who it is before she lets herself believe. Marcel and Seth turn in alarm when they hear the splash. Crea has dived into the water.

Mother and child meet in breathless embrace. The water churns around them while they shout, cry, laugh, scream, and do a dance in the waves.

O

Thanksgiving is celebrated in fervent gratitude for survival. The fever is gone, storm damage has been assessed and remedies are under way. The harvest has not been bad considering, and the weather is finally cooling. The long tables set up under the trees near the shore display fat squashes, beans, cornbread, pickles, fish, rabbit, lamb, dandelion greens, blackberries, apple and pumpkin pies, cider, roasted chestnuts, and bayberry wine. Against the murky November sky among the pines many trees are already bare, stripped by the storm; the remaining yellow leaves are browning, here and there a maple flaming red. A makeshift band plays cheerfully, including Fair and Seth on their harmonicas.

Crea and Marcel stand on the dock in a fresh lake breeze, clapping in time to the music. Her froth of blond hair is caught up loosely from her neck but escapes in careless twirls over her ears. With her white cotton dress, she's wearing a necklace of blue-green beads strung by Fair. Marcel's beard is trimmed short, he's black tan from outdoor exposure, deft craftsman's hands calloused. Tati comes striding down the hill, sees them, waves. They go to greet her.

"It's unbelievable," breathes Tati. They know she doesn't mean just the feast. "Unbelievable, mom!" Crea hugs her close.

Their soothing moment is grated sharply by a shout from Judge Vinsky calling the crowd to attention. He's not a judge, he didn't even go to law school, in fact he was trained as a chef and everybody knows it. But he likes the title, so he has it, no questions asked. In the chaos and terror of the double catastrophe, Vinsky's penchant for authority stood the community in good stead. Not only his strict rules about quarantine, contact and care of victims, but also setting up shelter and repair priorities, food distribution and preservation. The islanders have been acquiescent and grateful. He hasn't wanted to give up this power. In fact, he has solidified it. His aides have doubled in number and now carry clubs. There's talk of going to the mainland to forage for guns.

"Folks, folks, this is a great day! Look at what we've accomplished in the short six weeks since we got hit with that double whammy. Congratulations to all of us!" He stands feet wide apart on his stumpy legs, blue armband strapped around pudgy arm. "And now, I'd like to take this opportunity to announce my decision to forbid any more newcomers. We've been blessed lately with welcoming more of Tatyana's family, some great people. But in spite of our sad losses, the eighty-four souls here now are the max. You know our island's resources are limited. From now on, we'll have to turn people away. Long live Tully Island!"

"Hip, hip, hooray," yell his aides, but not many others.

"What happened to our community meetings?" seethes Tati. "That's not the way we decide things here."

"Looks like he's taken over permanently," observes Marcel.

Fair and Seth have come to join them and Seth chimes in sardonically, "He's got a good thing going."

Tati looks at her daughter and granddaughter, still hardly daring to believe they really are here with her at last, the agony of Leon's loss eased and sharpened at the same time. How he would have rejoiced with her!

Tati looks around with a dark lens of foreboding. The hills curving over the lake have glaring bald spots where trees were downed. Can they get to them in time to use them, or will the trees just rot? One small fishing boat has been rebuilt. Can they build another in time to feed all these people? So many homes have been damaged, how will they mend them all before winter? There's too much food on that table. Vinsky's a decisive and charismatic leader but he's short on wisdom and foresight: he's showing off. The lamb was one of the last, not a smart move when so many sheep drowned. The berries are gone until spring, the squash is dwindling. Soon another group of refugees will come. Will Vinsky succeed in driving them away without violence? What if they are better armed, fight back, take over? Will the fear never end? She wants to shout, "Stop celebrating, stop this charade! Wake up!" But of course she doesn't, smiles instead at her family's bright faces and only teases, "don't eat too much pumpkin pie."

Fair and Seth return to the band, playing a sprightly rendition of the old favorite, "Walk of Life," and Marcel and Crea clasp in a dance. Before she realizes what she's doing, Tati wanders off and finds herself in front of her house. Such an ugly little house, all black rubber and odd protuberances, and now lopsided to boot from wind damage. And their poor little outhouse in shambles. Marcel and Seth are working on both when they can, but Vinsky has assigned them to far more urgent projects. Her black-eyed daisies, seemingly immortal all summer, have mostly not survived the storm, so that only a few torn orange-gold blossoms are left amid the dried mud ridges. But there they are, nevertheless, roguish perks of color, and she's ridiculously glad to see them. She sits on a great rock facing her house.

The joy of Crea and Fair being here with her elusively and cruelly remains outside Tati's aching heart. Her heart barely thuds along, crushed with raging grief. Leon, Leon, she cries.

"What are we going to do?" she asks him. "Everything is such a mess. Everything is dangerous. Winter's coming, the food will run out, bandits will come, or others who want the island. I'm so scared, Leon."

The trees whisper, "Be strong."

But she doesn't want to be strong, not any more. She wants to shrivel fleshless, melt away.

When Crea was ten, Tati's father and wife Del came to Concord for Christmas, to see the new house. They'd just moved there from Long Island, full of confidence that Martin's professorship at Tufts would soon mean tenure. His demons had not yet overwhelmed him, and he was jolly with Ray. The men had long confabs about the sport of kayaking, which Ray had long given up and Martin never would actually try, but that didn't dampen their enthusiasm, their swaggering masculine embrace of the dangers, the details. Tati was torn between her pleasure in their camaraderie, and her being left thus to the devices of Del, who loudly proclaimed how to set the table, keep Crea quiet, arrange the Christmas decorations, renovate the kitchen, and correctly mash potatoes.

There had been no snow for a couple of years, but then it came. They were all sitting around watching TV, some innocuous show suitable for Crea, who cuddled on the couch next to her father, clutching her Polly dolly. Crea all spun gold and angelic rosyness, Martin too solid, unmovably solid, his broad shoulders going to fat. Ray already asleep in his chair, mouth agape, sorrowing Tati with the sight of his grayed skin, flabbed jowls, hands gnarled and veined. She had never imagined in all her past rage that the revenge of his old age would hurt her so.

The show was interrupted by a glamorous reporter looking appropriately shaken, who announced gale warnings. Tati went to the window.

"Wow," she reported, "the trees are blowing sideways. They're whipping around like crazy dancers."

"Snow! Snow! We can build a snowman," cried Crea. "I haven't seen snow since I was seven, right, daddy? Have we got a carrot for his nose?"

Tati watched the first flakes starting, small sharp intent dots, no artistry or softness there, dashing sidelong like threats. It looked like the kind of snow that never intends to stop. While they were still discussing what hat the snowman would wear, the lights went out. Everybody groaned, "not again!" Blackouts were already happening all the time; the one last month had lasted forty-eight hours. Tati wearily brought out the candles and battery-powered lamps.

Later on, since the gas stove still worked, they had a comfortable and comforting dinner. Everyone was especially nice to each other, mellowed at losing all their manmade conveniences. No TV, no phone, no toilet flushing, no faucet water, no radio, no computer. No heat. All those wonders they still took for granted in those days.

This time the blackout lasted for almost a week. For two days the snow piled up, so eventually they couldn't see out the first floor windows. Then came freezing rain, coating everything with heavy layers of ice. Large trees broke in half like twigs. The corpses of birds and squirrels splayed over ice piles, in poses of astonishment. Plows were not able to get through the roads. In the end they were all huddled in the kitchen by the stove, eating canned food and rationing the bottled water. Everyone except Martin, who would not get out of bed no matter how far the temperature dipped in their bedroom, who was never the same after that.

Even when the electricity came back on, Martin lay stony. Crea would come in and poke at him, beg him to talk to her. Then after a while she just stared at him, and finally she refused to go see him at all. Of course later he revived, got more medication, walked around and even made a go at teaching his classes. But his family always knew he wouldn't be there for long, and he was only a remembrance of himself in any case. Tati took care of everything. Everybody said, oh Tati is so strong. Crap, as Leon would say. She cried by herself many, many a night.

"Leon," she groans now, crouched with the pain of it on the rock on Tully Island, an old woman. "My soul, you took my soul with you. Come back! I want you back."

○

When Crea and Fair go off to see what's happened to Tati, Marcel and Seth watch them walking away, each savoring his lover's hips, saying to himself, just look at that dream of a woman. Then they turn to each other with smiles, knowing what the other was thinking.

Seth says, "Hey, that Vinsky needs a dose of reality."

"Don't even think about it. We just got here. We can't make trouble."

"He's the one making trouble."

Marcel agrees but doesn't say so. He glowers at the younger man, aware that for this surly brave heart, settling down and abiding by rules won't be easy.

So he reasons, "Let's take the temperature of this place first, check out the whole situation. Move, if we move, from a position of strength."

The conspiracy vocabulary soothes Seth, as his friend knew it would.

"Keep our heads down for now," concedes Seth, with a brotherly slap on the back.

Crea puts her arm around Fair as they walk, and after a while Fair puts hers around Crea too. They step carefully over the deep ruts that were just recently rivers of mud, maneuver past fallen trees and debris.

Crea says, "I love you sweetpea. I'm the luckiest woman in the world."

Fair is quiet. She has vaguely recognized her mother's new self-confidence, senses her deepened strength and peace. But she doubts that this translates into awareness of her child as a person. She fears Crea still thinks of her as an ignorant coddled fifteen-year-old. Fair hopes she can get her to understand that what she's been through has changed her forever, has made her into a woman hardened and distrustful, fierce and possessive and a fighter.

"Mom," she tries. Stops, so they face each other. "Mom, I love you but I need you to see who I am now."

Crea gazes at her entranced. "I'm trying, sweetie. You are a fantastic woman. I'm so proud of you."

Fair knows her mother hasn't perceived the half of it, but this is enough for now. They climb the hill and look down at Tati hunched on the rock, head in hands.

Tati looks up to see them hurrying towards her. She stands up and for a moment her dulled eyes unshutter. She opens her arms.

Episode 12

Others

Here he comes, old Dr. Dom, toddling along on his cane down the hill. Tati watches from where she sits outside her door, feet propped up to rest her tired legs. He's got a remarkably lush head of white hair, and his drooping pink face is strong, the inroads of experience defying debility. His stomach is a paunch but his limbs are skinny. He waves a bony arm in her direction.

"Stew for supper," she tells him. "And I picked some lettuce."

He kisses her on the lips, drops into the chair beside her. They sit hand in hand looking out at the lake.

It's a nice May evening. The latest heat wave subsided days ago, so the slight breeze off the water smells a little fresher. The barren extension of the shore is sprouting grasses and tiny trees in cracked soil, and the sea of algae swarming the edge of the lake is yards thick now, but beyond that the water sparkles just as it always has.

"We'll have some of my jam tart for dessert, shall we?" he says. Then, because she doesn't answer and he knows what she's waiting for, he continues, "Crea's not doing so well today, I'm afraid."

"Yes. I noticed this morning she's been bleeding again."

"I don't know what more I can do."

"She's improved before. Maybe this is just another phase she'll get through."

He squeezes her hand. "It is another phase."

"Dominick, don't lie to me."

"I just don't know if she'll get better. With chronic leukemia, it could go on for years. I just don't know."

"Is Fair there now?"

"She's upstairs feeding Orion, but she'll be in and out. Don't worry about that. Crea has everything she needs."

For a while they are quiet. Dom lets go of her hand to trace her forehead with his fingers, brushing back her hair. His tenderness stifles her despair. Crea could live for years: that will have to do as good news.

"How are the other patients? Did you and Fair have a satisfactory day?"

"We did. Especially with the children. Having all the kids together now in that room at the big house works wonders for their spirits. The asthmatics have improved so much in these last few days with the weather, a few of them have been able to go home for some family time." Dom squints out over the lake. "It looks clear enough, we might get another day or so of clean air."

"That would be great. Aren't we lucky Orion's lungs are ok!"

"Yup. I think now he's turned two, chances are he'll be fine."

Tati stops herself from saying, "but who knows what else might afflict him." So many of the children are sick or disabled, many of them born that way but others suddenly, out of rosy health, struck at various ages with everything from cancer to nerve disorders. And there aren't enough of them any more. Fertility is way down. Dom says it's mostly the endocrine disrupters, the estrogen mimics in the water, interfering with reproduction. This may also be why there are so few wild animals left. Or maybe people just had to eat them all. The stew on her stove right now owes its heartiness to squirrel parts.

She says, "Orion looks so much like Seth, sturdy and dark. And stubborn. Fair's happy about that, but still. Sort of makes it harder."

"It's that stubbornness got him shot, out on that expedition. Let's hope Orion isn't so headstrong. Seth just had to go and be a hero. There was no need for it!"

"He was brave," cries Tati. "Don't you put him down for that. He might even have saved his friends' lives. You know, if he hadn't drawn their fire...you've got to at least give Fair that consolation."

"It's been almost a year since he died." Dom skirts her emotion with pragmatism. "Fair's pretty much regained her equilibrium."

"Outwardly. She hasn't stopped mourning, really. Maybe never will."

"Ah, we all do. Even you."

Tati turns to smile at him. "You're my knight in shining armor."

"A bit creaky," he laughs.

Tati goes inside to tend the stew, mix up some dandelion greens with the lettuce, toss them with sunflower oil and cider vinegar. The violets she picked yesterday perk in their vase on the table. Out the window coming around the bend from the woods she sees Marcel and Vinsky marching along with some of their band, including Miles, all armed now with guns. They stop to talk to Dom. She listens to their voices, brusque and urgent. The air tightens in her throat. Trouble.

When she comes out, Marcel is saying, "...now they're asking to share the water supply on the east side."

"That can't happen," states Vinsky.

"They're only asking," Marcel reasons.

Dom interjects, "There are more of them now than us. Maybe we should recruit like they do."

"We don't have the food, you know that," Marcel points out.

"They don't either," Vinsky snorts. "That's why they're after ours."

"They only want water," Miles braves, backing up Marcel.

Miles has grown into a hefty broad-shouldered man, his boy's round freckled face squared and darkened. Like all the men, he sports a beard, short and bushy, lighter brown than the hair on his head. The beard rescues his short neck and big ears, Tati thinks, and decides proudly that he looks quite handsome. She knows him to be a kind man, too sensitive perhaps for all the pain he has seen, and too kind surely for the pain to come.

She quickly says, "You're negotiating, right? No need to threaten them."

"Right," agrees Marcel, nodding to her. "And they know we're much better armed."

Marcel is leaner than ever, too lean, his dark hair thickly streaked with gray. Crea's illness has taken the light from his eyes, made him gaunt and bitter. But anger no longer controls him. Instead, his fight for the common good is lit by sadness, by tolerance if not resignation.

"For now," Vinsky mutters.

Vinsky on the other hand is even more belligerent than before. He shares power with Marcel and others reluctantly and resentfully.

Marcel says to Tati, "Are you coming by this evening?"

"Of course," she says.

"See you then."

The little band marches off, uniform only in their frayed blue armbands, pistols at waists or rifles over shoulders, dusty and unmilitary in their tired gait.

"God," moans Tati looking after them, "I hope there won't be any killing."

"Hey," growls Dom, "those types who've settled over there on the other side of Tully, they're a band of ruffians. They don't have any scruples. Don't be blind. We're going to have to deal with them."

"What does deal with them mean," she queries defiantly, standing in front of him. "You sound as bad as Vinsky."

Dom looks up at her from where he sits, amusement in his eyes. "You keep us in line," he replies, a smile pulling at his lips. "Nobody gets hurt when you're around."

"Dominick, don't you patronize me!"

Hands on hips, she pulls herself up tall and fierce.

"Hey," he says, "you win."

She turns her back and strides off, sits down on the boulder glaring at him from a distance.

"I'm going to wash up," he tells her mildly, and goes into the house.

As soon as he's out of sight, she wants to hurry after him. But she sits glumly on the rock, shadows cast by the lowering sun lengthening.

○

At the same time, Fair puts Orion in his crib, where he putters with toys for a minute and then starts to yell. So she takes him out again and carries him onto the porch. This used to be the deck of the yacht the Zorians brought here years ago. Seth and Marcel transformed the boat into two homes. Downstairs Crea and Marcel live in the space that includes the berth area, and Fair and Orion have two comfortable rooms above. The porch faces the dock where the fishing boats sway, their masts clanking.

One is docking right now, with Kiva and her husband and brother scampering to ease it in and tie it up. Looks like they have a good catch. The fish in the tub are all small, of course. The bigger ones are too shot with mercury and other accumulated toxins to be safely eaten any more. The problem with that is, the young are often being caught before they reproduce, so on top of oxygen getting choked off by algae, fish in Lake Willoughby are diminishing. Farm fishing is being tried in a small inland pond, with some success so far. Other sources of protein are a constant search these days. Some people have begun gathering insects, of which there are many because the birds have dwindled. People in the kitchen are developing creative recipes to disguise reality. For example, Stella has invented a paste made from ants and termites that eerily resembles peanut butter. She calls it "fairy butter" and the kids at least are fooled.

Kiva waves from the boat. In her ragged shorts and sleeveless shirt, with her sun darkened skin and long limbs, she looks as she gestures, casts rope, clambers the mast, furls sails, like an exotic dancer.

"Orion, Orie, see Kiva," says Fair. "Hi, Kiva," making his hand wave back.

Orion cries out, "Kiva, Kiva come here! Play with Orie, Kiva."

Fair hugs him until he squeals and writhes to be put down, then he runs to the railing, laughing. Watching him she thinks yet again, the way she draws breath, of Seth. How proud he was of his son, how loving and protective. She herself in Seth's arms, where nothing could hurt her. Instead, she and little Orion left behind here on this earth without him, vulnerable and alone. Orion's hair is exactly the stiff deep black of his father's, and his big dark eyes mirror the man's. When she looks into her child's face sometimes she comes to tears seeing there his father's soul gleaming back to her.

After one more attempt at the crib, Fair gives up and decides to take Orion with her downstairs to visit her mother.

"I tried to get him to sleep but no dice," she apologizes to Crea. "I hope he doesn't exhaust us both."

Crea's face beams. "No, it's good. I want to see him. Orion, come to granny."

She's sitting among pillows in a reclining chair between two round windows, one overlooking the lake, the other in sight of a large vegetable garden, fields of wheat and corn beyond. Placed where his grandmother can hold him, Orion twists away and runs immediately to the cupboard where he begins taking out pots and pans to make a symphony. Fair lures him from that with a cookie and a pile of blocks, so for a little while he lets them talk.

Crea's face is white. So is her hair, which has thinned and coarsened. Her arms on the sheet are loose fleshed with muscle loss. Fair checks for blood, feels her forehead.

"A little better?"

"Better, sweetpea. You know it's usually not so bad this time of day. Sunset is good for me."

"Tell me about when I was two," starts Fair, offering the ritual salve of the past. "Was I a handful like Orie?"

"Pretty much," smiles Crea. "You were a feisty little girl, defiant and disobedient sometimes, you know. Spoiled. Just like Orion. But, listen. I want to talk about something else. I've been thinking about this for days."

Fair pulls up a chair and takes her mother's hand. "Sure, mom."

"It's about Miles."

"He's so good with Orion. I know. You think I shouldn't make him babysit so much? Maybe I…"

Crea squeezes her hand. "No, no, that's all right. He loves Orion, that's just it. I'm having trouble expressing…I'm afraid you'll be mad at me. But even if you are, listen anyway please."

Fair stands up, leans on the back of the chair, and gets ready for something annoying, nodding with encouragement she does not feel. Two bright rose spots come to Crea's cheeks with the effort and excitement.

"Miles is a grown man now," Crea pursues. "He's twenty — only four years younger than you, remember. Sweetpea, he likes you. No, let me finish. I'm only asking, give him the respect of recognizing him as a man, and stop treating him like a boy. I know, I know. He's like your little brother in your mind. But he's not your brother. He's not little. He's grown up. He needs a woman."

Fair stares at her mother, who has fallen back on the pillows out of breath.

"Mom, you are way off base on this one," she says evenly. "Miles is just a kid, and then there's the small matter of Seth, in case you forgot."

Exhausted with her effort, Crea shakes her head slowly. "Seth is gone," she whispers.

"What?"

"I said, Seth is gone."

"No he's not. He's here in my heart." Fair pounds her chest with a fist. "He's in every inch of Orie. How can you be so cruel?"

Crea was prepared for this attack. That's why she rehearsed her idea over and over, and why she put off broaching it a dozen times. But what she is surprised by is her own hurt. It's unbearable to have Fair so upset with her. Struggling with physical pain all the time, confronting it, bargaining with it, living with this enemy inside her, she has no stomach for fighting anything else.

So she only limply replies. "I want you to be taken care of," which is the worst possible thing she could say to Fair.

"Taken care of? What? I've been taking care of myself since I was fifteen, you know that. Nobody has to take care of Fair Franklin!"

"I mean…"

"Never mind, mom." Fair's face has softened, but not her eyes. She's contrite at her mother's distress, but her anger still flames. "I know you mean well. I love you too." She comes to smooth the pillows, rearrange the blanket over her mother's legs. "I've got to take Orie up and get him to sleep. Gran will come by to see you soon. Do you need anything? How about more tea?"

Left alone, Crea realizes she's crying again. The tears wet her neck before she's aware they have come. It seems that nothing in her life has turned out as she hoped, including her own self. She had wanted strength and integrity, but has weakly given in and compromised, too many times. As for Fair, she used to assume her daughter would become cultured, elegant, serene, soft-spoken. But Fair is none of those things. She buzzes about in overalls, her short hair uncombed, her voice edged with sarcasm and defiance. Her education truncated, her vast musical promise reduced to tooting on a harmonica! Towards Fair, even deep in mother's love, Crea feels more awe than pride, and a certain resentment. Since she's been sick, she's found it even harder to accept that her child has grown and gone, is no longer hers. She craves the satisfaction of being needed, but instead sees herself an appendage, supported and giving no support. Marcel, when she voiced this despair, vociferously denied it and almost wept in begging her to accept how much he relies on her. But really, he doesn't. He's intense with his strategies and forays, meetings and speeches. She can't even any longer give him her body, the warrior's solace.

Upstairs, holding Orion and crooning to calm him down, Fair watches Miles come down the hill from the main house. It's his usual time. He'll stay with Orion while she goes to help Kiva clean the fish for tomorrow. Her mother's right about one thing — Miles has grown up. He's at least six feet tall and moves like a bulldozer. To Fair it has seemed a bit pretentious for a boy so young to act so manly, but now for the first time she recognizes how natural it is. She feels a confusion of maternal pride, sisterly concern, and womanly admiration. Fair doesn't like or expect to be confused. She shakes her head in annoyance.

"Myley!" shrieks Orion, stretching out his pudgy arms.

Miles sweeps him up, tosses him around, laughs deeply. "Not in bed yet? Giving your mother a hard time?"

Fair tidies up the kitchen area, splashes cold water on her face, runs a comb through her hair. On the spur of the moment she decides to change her shirt. Why should she want to look nicer to go and clean fish? The question is never fully formed. In the bedroom through the closed door she hears Miles and Orion having a serious discussion, smiles, sees her smile in the mirror, keeps it as she finishes taking off her shirt. She pauses to look at her breasts in the dim light. Behind her she can see the bed, the big wonderful bed Seth made for them, lovingly crafted in spare time he didn't have. Seth's hands smoothing and testing the wood, his hands on her face, his hands and arms and hips. She fingers her nipples, watching her mouth come open at the sensation.

Just before he left that last time, Seth had been so attentive to them both, Orion then still an infant. His usual abrupt manner was softened, even with others. He was all love. At least that's how she remembers it, how she has replayed it thousands of times in her yearning mind. But the goodbye at the dock had been routine. Seth going off with Marcel and others to barter for oxygen for the asthmatics, new drinking water filters, ammunition, other staples like salt and soap. No sense of dread accompanied their last kisses. And everyone did come back safe and sound, everyone except Seth. That was the greatest bitterness.

Pulling on her pink flowered blouse, welcoming its cool softness, Fair suddenly is aware of Miles' voice singing. He's always singing to Orion. He sings with the band. He even sings when he's repairing something. But she has never really heard his voice before. Its beauty freezes her in mid action, fingertips twisting a button. The timbre of the bass is resonant, full, angelic. She pauses there, swept over by the music, staring at her own startled flushed face, in a long moment that changes everything. When she goes back out to the other room, she doesn't dare to meet his eyes, but she touches his shoulder in departing with a hand that trembles.

O

Tati makes her way after supper up the hill into the woods. She's headed for the fish pond, but on the way as always she takes a small detour to the cemetery. As she passes through gardens and fields she glories in the bounty of May. Last year at this time they'd endured a killer frost that mutilated half the crops, but this year looks like it might be a winner. The corn is almost knee high, tomatoes reddening, herbs and beans healthy. She stoops at one plot to admire radishes pushing up plump crimson tops. She pulls one out, brushes it off, bites into its earth-warm spice.

The cemetery is not organized by individuals. There's not enough land for that. There are just rows of large stones, each bearing a name. Some of the stones march across mounds, where many people had to be buried at once. It's a peaceful spot, open to the sky but surrounded by unbroken green. She sits down beside Leon. A daisy she brought yesterday still reclines across the letters of his name. She doesn't talk to him much any more. Dom is her confidante now. But she doesn't come here out of duty either. Rather she's drawn by the finality and eternity, the sense of ending. The roundness of completed life.

She slips off her sandals and stretches her legs out straight, contemplating the knots of varicose veins. Once upon a time her legs were slim and smooth. These legs have seen a lot of love. Walked a lot of paths. Games with her brother Ned in the broad back yard and along the sweeping Cape Cod beaches, now all gone. Trips with her dizzy mother to buy her first bra, her first prom gown. Then everything darkening with her father's departure; the boys in back seats who did not compensate. Graduate school, her first taste of professional importance. Martin, her first love, their astonishing passion; her baby, and everything transformed to a lens filled only with little Crea. Martin going, away into his own dungeon world; Crea going, away into adolescence and off to college. Tati's affairs, their relief, their moments of unlikely joy, the wrench of their ending. The growing horror of the environmental holocaust, the dawning knowledge that it would never get better — only far, far worse. Reconciling with her father, loving him again only to face his interminable dying. Leon's coming to her and into her, intoxicating escape. Trying to reach Crea and Canada, the refugee camp, the deaths, the suffering, the perseverance, the wildly improbable moments of happiness and hope. Leon's cruel going, where she can never reach him again.

The earth is dry and still hot. She burrows her legs and feet into it. Some day she will lie here too, and a stone will bear her name.

At the pond, Abram and his young son are preparing the feed and she pitches in. The setting sun breaks through haze and pinks the water. On the other side of the pond the trees are already darkening.

The fish farm is a favorite project of Tati's, mostly because the majority of the Tully community has given up on it. The pond has already had to be re-stocked twice. First the trout died, in one fell swoop going belly up, all of them. Catfish have been more successful, but the older adults are growing suspicious lesions, so that now they have to harvest the juveniles and younger adults just to be safe. But Tati is stubbornly committed to making this project work. For one thing, the quality of the water is so much better than in the lake, and they can monitor and adjust it.

But today she notes a little pile of corpses.

"They turned up dead just this afternoon," Abram tells her.

The catlike whiskers distorted, gills swollen, discolored patches. Toxins have reached even here. Thinking, let's hope the younger fish are not affected, she also knows that if the water is tainted, all the creatures in it are at risk, and anyone who eats them is too.

Trying not to strain her back, she helps lift the pipe across, Abram's bare arms pulsing with effort beside hers. She pauses to push sweat away from her eyes and in that instant catches a glimpse of something crouching in the shadowed trees on the other side. Her shock makes her lose her grip.

"Watch it!" Abram yells as he catches the pipe just in time.

"Look," she says very quietly.

He ignores her. He and his son lock the pipe into place and nod to each other with satisfaction. Tati grips his arm. He follows her eyes and sees what she sees: a row of faces.

Yes, they are human. They are very still in their watching like animals, and their eyes are wide with wanting, but their faces are intelligent, calculating. Even though they are different sizes, they all look alike from here — skeletal and dark. Now they are coming forward out of the woods, moving cautiously but purposefully towards the shore. Clothed in colorless rags, they are so thin their shoulders and knees jut bones. They have guns.

Abram pushes his son behind him. "Get the shotgun," he hisses. "In the shed."

As Abram's son starts running, the people on the shore raise their weapons and fire. Tati finds herself flat on the ground where Abram has thrown her. They wiggle backwards towards the shelter of the shed. Abram gets to his knees to fire the shotgun and two of the strange apparitions fall, collapsing into shapeless heaps. But now he's spouting blood and Tati grabs the gun. At first she aims for legs. Surely the sound of gunfire will bring all of Tully running to the rescue any minute. But one of the skeletons keeps coming, firing from the hip. She presses the gun to her shoulder and aims for his heart.

When he drops, the rest of them scatter, fade back into the trees. Behind her she hears Marcel shouting, she hears beloved voices crying out, she watches Abram being tended, his son comforted, feels arms around her. But she frees herself and heads for the other side of the pond, to the bodies. She gazes down at the man she has killed. His blood is reddening and bubbling the dust. His astonished eyes are wide open. No doubt all he wanted was food. No doubt he was courageous, a leader, probably a lover, maybe had children. She has taken his life away.

His beard and hair are curly, honey blond beneath the grime. His smiling mouth, where the teeth are becoming subsumed with blackish blood, seems on the verge of speech. Did he say someone's name as he died? His calloused slender hands are thrown out at his sides in open surrender. Tati studies the hairs of his eyebrows, the curl of his inner ear, the veins of his neck and nose, the symmetrical outline of his ribs. He hadn't been taking such a risk. One man, an old woman, and a boy should have been easy to vanquish. His people would have had fish to feast on.

"I'm sorry," she tells him, repeats it in sobs over and over.

She turns to look back at her own people, the faces she knows so well, the lives intertwined with hers. The killing has begun. Precious Tully will run with blood. She thinks, this is what we have become, this is what I have become.

She watches with blurred eyes the last ridge of the sun slip below the hills. Darkness will gather quickly now.

Acknowledgements

I would like to thank family and friends for their inspiration and support, especially Frances Beer, Samuel H. Beer, Sasha Pearson, Helen Snively, and Alison Woodman.

I am also grateful to my nurturing and diligent writers' group.

Excerpts from this novel first appeared in *Facets* magazine and Harvard's *HILR Review*.

About the Author

Kitty Beer's stories and articles have appeared in print and online in the U.S. and Canada, including her work as an environmental journalist. Her screenplay, *Home*, placed in the 2004 PAGE International Screenwriting Awards contest. She is a member of the National Writers Union, PEN New England, and the Society of Environmental Journalists.

Kitty Beer grew up in New England and raised her two children in Canada, Germany, and upstate New York. She holds her B.A. from Harvard University, and her M.A. from Cornell University. She now makes her home in Cambridge, Massachusetts. *What Love Can't Do* is her first novel. She is currently at work on a sequel.

About the Artist

Susan Cohen Thompson's watercolor painting "Earth Singing to Herself" is from a series of paintings envisioning humans reconnected with nature. The theme of interconnectedness runs through all of Thompson's works. Previously from Massachusetts, she now resides on an island north of Seattle, Washington. Visit her website for more of her work: www.thompsonartstudio. com.